SWITCHBLADE

Edited by Scotch Rutherford

Switchblade, Issue Sixx, Volume One
First Printing, August 2018

ISBN-13: 978-0-9987650-6-8
ISBN-10: 0998765066

©2018 Caledonia Press

www.switchblademag.com

The following stories are works of fiction. All of the names, characters, organizations, corporations, institutions, events, and locations portrayed in these works are either products of the author's imagination, or, if real, used fictitiously. The resemblance of any character to actual persons (dead or alive), are purely coincidental.

SEATTLE

He said he's trying to get home to see his boy,
knows the city like he knows loss, and brother,
he's lost it all.

Spire on the horizon, retro-futurist
palace in pink clouds.

Looking for life on a Broadway strip but finding
a thousand kinds of death dressed in rags
with bags on their backs and chemical eyes.

Cop a sack of glass from a kid with a can
with a false bottom, blast off beside a dumpster,
break the shackles of gravity—

pinging   blips on a radar screen
                         above roads   skipping scenes
                    the voices singing
                                     bodies
                                              human percussion of
                crashing   atoms
                                    in parks and alleys
                          in the wide open
                     stalking sidewalks
                for a place to set up
                          a place to trade these songs
                                for silver
                     our collision of limbs
                stripped fingers grieving snapped
          E's and G strings pulling notes from on high or low
to fill the spaces till   coins pile into wine
and faces   places led and followed to   erratic procession
     each car riding   deep   to where the street meets water
                          lights like drowning stars

CONTENTS

The girl with the Switchblade tattoo is Demi Cobar. In case you were wondering, and I know you were. Ask anyone who knows me personally, and they'll tell you I'm Low Status, Uncouth, and Broke. But in the same breath, they'll tell you I know a lot of beautiful women. There's something to be said about anyone who counts himself as an angry bottom feeder on the ragged edge. People with less to loose, can afford to take risks. I've heard that all goes away when you make it to the folding money. You might consider Ellery Queen the top tier of crime fiction periodicals—showing up there, might be like playing Carnegie Hall. And if so, getting your name in this rag would be like playing to the mosh pit at CBGBs...

And let's face it, that right there pushes the needle into the red on the cool factor gauge. Speaking of the golden age of punk, Rex Weiner has a story in this issue. Nobody in this issue knows that scene better than Rex, who first serialized *The Adventures of Ford Fairlane* in *The New York Rocker* in 1979, and *The LA Weekly*, back in '81, long before it became a film featuring shock comic Andrew Dice Clay. In fact, Rex started writing about the rock and roll detective back when Dice was still making his bones at *Pips* in Brooklyn, and still calling himself Andy Silverstein. If you know me, you know I like Dice, about half as much asI like Sam Kinisen, and a fifth as much as I like Lenny Bruce—who I like *almost as much* as I despise censorship,and political correctness. This issue also marks *Tough* Editor, Rusty Barnes' long awaited *Switchblade* debut. MikePayne, John Bosworth, Evelyn Deshane, Jim Thomsen, G Garnet, Scot Carpenter, and Aidan Thorn join Switchblade vets EF Sweetman, Travis Richardson, Danny Sophabmisay, Tom Barlow, and Tais Teng. The following 14 hard luck tales are razor sharp, spring loaded, and under extreme tension—this is Switchblade Issue Sixx, and it's another robust issue. Who says more than a handful is too much?

——Scotch Rutherford
　(Managing Editor)

The (Original) Adventures of Ford Fairlane

The Long Lost Rock 'n' Roll Detective Stories

Before the movie about a rock n' roll detective there were Rex Weiner's noirish stories, capturing the punk rock 1970s in New York and Los Angeles in all their gritty glory...

First published in the New York Rocker and the LA Weekly in 1979- 1980, the stories became the basis for the 20th Century Fox motion picture starring Andrew Dice Clay. From CBGBs, the Mudd Club and Tier 3 in NYC to the Starwood, Zero Zero and Cuckoo's Nest in LA, Ford Fairlane takes you back to a sexy, violent and explosively creative time and place that live on in rock n' roll legend, brought authentically to life in these hardboiled stories, published by Rare Bird Books. In bookstores now!

"With Tom Waits like prose, you'll be out-hipped."
—John Densmore, *The Doors*

QUICK & DIRTY

FLASH ⚡ FICTION
FLASH ⚡ FICTION
FLASH ⚡ FICTION
FLASH ⚡ FICTION
FLASH ⚡ FICTION
FLASH ⚡ FICTION
FLASH ⚡ FICTION

Down Payment

George Garnet

Before knocking on the door, the woman's eyes briefly slide over the dimly lit motel's parking lot. She instantly recognizes the black Cadillac parked next to a beat up Ford.

The woman gently squeezes the little boy's hand and whispers, "Remember what I said?"

"Yeah, Mom." The boy holds tight on to his mom's warm palm.

She straightens the collar of his *Superman* jacket and adjusts his plastic water toy gun strapped across his shoulder. Holding her breath she knocks on the door and listens.

The door opens an inch and a beefy man's face peers through the gap. His podgy eyes shift down on the woman's deep cleavage, down her miniskirt, her thighs, her bright red high heels.

"Yeah?" he says with a husky voice.

"Donna to see Mr. Barkley."

The door opens wider.

"Who's this?" He points a meaty finger at the boy.

"That's my son Clayton. He is seven and that's why I couldn't leave him home alone..."

The slightly crossed man's eyes remind the mother and her son of Mr. Colsten, the boarding school principal.

While stepping aside, his solid body wobbling, the man points with his head for them to move inside. When they pass by, he shuts the door and stands behind them, thick arms crossed.

The room is small with a bed in the middle, and curtains tightly closed. The smell of mold and disinfectant mix in the air. Sitting on the edge of the bed an old man in a dark suit and a black hat stares at the visitors without blinking. Suddenly his thin, pencil-drawn moustache curls as he smiles.

"Ah, Donna, sweetheart, where—"

"I'm sorry, Mr. Barkley for the late payment, I'm—" The woman interrupts him with trembling voice.

"Sure, sure, sweetheart. But you're already two days late." He pats an aluminum case lying next to him on the bed. "The down payment was for Tuesday—"

"So sorry, Mr. Barkley, I got the money in my purse—" The woman's voice breaks down as if she is expecting to be punched.

"Cranky." Mr. Barkley nods at the solid man.

Cranky snatches the woman's purse.

"Your son is real cute, Donna. Is that a water gun strapped across his shoulder?" Mr. Barkley can't take his eyes off the little boy.

"He thinks he is my protector. " The woman tries a short laugh that comes out phony. "Like on that TV commercial, when a little boy threatens an intruder with his buccaneer's sword. It's very funny, I bet you've seen it, Mr. Barkley."

"Sure, he's a real guard of his mother. What a cute little man —" Mr. Barkley keeps staring at the boy.

"It's three hundred short," Cranky grunts suddenly and raises his eyebrow still holding the woman's purse.

Mr. Barkley looks at the woman, his eyes narrow now. He leans forward. "What would you do if someone owed you money, Donna?"

The woman quivers, her face drawn. "I'm getting old, Mr. Barkley. Men are looking for young women nowadays..."

As Cranky grabs her by the hair and pulls back, the woman shrieks. The startled boy searches for his mom's eyes, his little hand on the water gun.

"Maybe it's time for you to retire, honey? Or—" Mr. Barkley pauses for a long moment while he is playing with his leather glove. "How about young Clayton here? I have an idea—"

"Not that, Mr. Barkley! Please, not that!" The woman cries out and the boy's skin prickles.

"I think little Clayton can help you with your debt."

With an effort the woman turns her head in the boy's direction. Their eyes meet. How beautifully black are his mother's eyes, the boy thinks. Her big eyes blink rapidly now.

The boy swings his water gun from behind his back and points it at Cranky.

"What a dedicated bodyguard! I like that." Mr. Barkley laughs and slaps the aluminum case with his glove.

The boy's mother blinks rapidly again: that's two times.

Tightening his grip over the toy, as he has practiced many times before, the boy squeezes the trigger. The plastic barrel of the toy explodes as the strapped inside .38 revolver bangs loud and the recoil slams his shoulder. The bullet strikes Cranky's head and red mist bursts in the air spattering the woman's face.

"What the—" Mr. Barkley's eyes freeze as Cranky's body falls heavily to the floor.

The boy points the gun at Mr. Barkley.

"Donna! What—" Swallowing hard, the stunned old man struggles to find his words.

"Retirement, Mr. Barkley," she says in a tired voice.

The woman blinks again and the boy pulls the trigger. Another blast and Mr. Barkley's chest explodes. His limp body slides off the bed. The boy is still pointing his water gun at the lifeless old body when the woman lunges at him and hugs him tight. "You just saved your mama, baby," she whispers in his ear while keeping him pressed to her body. "You can let go of your water gun now."

The boy drops his gun and searches for his mom's hands. She lifts and sits him on the bed next to the aluminum case. When she opens it, inside, neatly stacked are thick wads of notes. They haven't seen so much money except on the TV. Weakness invades her legs and the woman lowers herself on the bed. "We're rich, very rich, sonny. You won't be shooting your water gun no more, babe."

She collects the wallets of the dead men and drops them inside the case. When she finishes washing her hands and face in the bathroom, she straps the water gun across the boy's shoulder and lifts the case.

"Give me your hand, my brave little man."

When they leave the room quietly, outside, in the thick darkness, the corner light looks like a glimmer in a tunnel.

***

©2018 George Garnet

Hooked

Aidan Thorn

"Well, thank you Maria. I'll see you again sometime."
He would bet the money he'd just paid her, and then some, that her name wasn't Maria but it was all he had. It felt a bit awkward now, was he supposed to kiss her.

"I look forward to it, Martin." Not his real name either.

Her short black dressing gown fell lose. A deliberate ploy, a final glimpse to encourage repeat custom? With one hand on his back she patted him and with a well practiced move opened the unlocked door with the other hand before putting just enough force into the one on his back to tell him it was time to go. No kiss, they were into another hour now—he'd only paid for one. He looked back to her as he stepped onto concrete. She forced a smile that said, *come on mister that's enough get out of here.* She shut the door.

As he'd done when he'd approached the house, he hunched into his clothes and pulled his hat down. He was overdressed for the weather. He looked both ways checking the street was clear.

It wasn't.

They were on him before he could react. A punch to the side of his face sent him to the pavement. A rain of kicks kept him there. He tried to cover up but the blows came fast.

"That's enough, get him up."

The kicking stopped. Rough hands dragged him to his feet, holding him where his legs wouldn't. He kept his eyes shut fearing that opening them would reveal the devil himself. There were at least three attackers, those holding him up and another who's stale tobacco breath was in his face.

"Open your eyes."

He felt the words leave the mouth of the man in front of him in a low menacing voice. He did as instructed. Their noses were almost touching. He recoiled in shock and his head cracked into a wall.

A low cackle from the face in front was echoed by those on either side. They were young, early twenties, but they were strong. Gym muscle obvious under tight fitted t-shirts.

"Wallet and phone." The face in front demanded. "Give him back his arms boys, he'll need to go in his pockets."

He fell against the wall and slumped to the pavement. The man in front of him took a step backwards and crouched into a squat bringing him back to eye-level. He repeated his demand.

"Wallet and phone."

He couldn't control the shake in his hand as he moved to pull his phone from his right jean pocket. It shook in his hand as he offered it.

"Thank you." The crouched attacker said as he took it and handed it up to one of his partners.

The other shaking hand went into the left jean pocket. As he pulled the wallet out a metallic ping cut through the air. The panic that had been etched on his face was nothing compared to that that was there now. He dropped the wallet and covered the object that had dropped.

The crouched attacker picked up the wallet.

"Lift up your hand."

"Please…no… please." His broken voice pathetic.

The attacker looked up to his right. He gave a nod and a standing kick was sent into the broken man's side. Instinct forced his arm up to cover the blow. A grin spread across the crouched attacker's face. He reached out and grabbed the wedding ring from the floor.

"Don't take it, please."

"You'd be in a lot of trouble if that went missing I imagine."

He didn't answer. The despair on his face told its own story.

The attacker opened the wallet pulling out the driving license.

"I'll tell you what, *David Peter Reid*. We'll let you keep the ring but you have to do something for us, OK?"

David nodded, desperate.

"The whore you just fucked. Did you see where she put your money?"

David's mind flashed back to an hour before. He'd handed over the money in the hallway and she'd opened a bureau drawer and put the money inside.

"It's in the hallway, in a drawer."

"And did you see if there was more in there."

"I think so… yes."

David couldn't be sure. He'd been nervous barely taking his eyes of the woman who went by Maria.

"OK, well thank you David."

He rifled through the wallet and pocketed the cash and bank cards as well as the drivers license. The empty wallet was dropped into David's lap. He held the wedding ring out between them. David tentatively reached for it. It was snatched away.

"No, I think I'll keep it. Now fuck off."

David pleaded. Tears welled in his eyes.

"Shut him the fuck up."

A blow to the head knocked David out.

"Wait here." The crouched attacker instructed the other two.

He walked to the door that David had left a few minutes before and knocked. Maria opened the door doing little to protect her modesty with the dressing gown that hung lose off of her.

"What did we get?" She asked.

"A few cards, about 90 quid, a phone and a wedding ring."

"Really, he wasn't wearing one."

"Fell out of his pocket, didn't it?"

Maria raised her eyebrows. She pulled him towards her kissing him. He grabbed for her ass as she lifted a leg and wrapped it around him.

"Come here you," She said pulling on his t-shirt, "Did he give up where I keep the money?"

"Yeah."

"Piece of shit."

*

The sun flickered through the trees casting short shadows on the grass. David wore sunglasses; they hid some of the bruising and tears. His head was bowed, it still hurt to stand. His cracked ribs strained as he let out a sigh and looked to the trees above. He brushed grey stone with a gentle hand.

"I'm sorry." He whispered as he turned from his late wife's grave and left the flowers he'd brought behind.

***

©2018 Aidan Thorn

On the Way Home

Rex Weiner

Friday, the end of a long week, and I'm collecting my things to go home when Walter from accounting comes over, stands by my desk, smiling in his chubby-faced way. Something funny happened to him the other day, he says.

He was at the mall, walking from his car towards the store through the parking lot when he saw a woman having trouble with her shopping cart. This part of the lot was on an incline. She was an older woman, all by herself, trying to push her cart, heavy with groceries, uphill. Each time she pushed, the cart rolled back down. She appeared to have given up altogether when Walter approached and asked if she was okay?

"I lost my husband," she said.

"I'm sorry," said Walter, feeling her grief. He took hold of the front of the cart. He pulled and she pushed, and together they rolled the cart up to a level spot, where they paused. The woman thanked Walter. Then she said, "Oh, there's my husband."

Spooked, Walter looked and saw a pickup truck with a man at the wheel driving towards them across the lot. He was waving at the woman.

"And I thought that, haha, you know," he says. "Lost her husband."

I laugh along with him and say that was a funny story. A few more items go into my briefcase.

"You think that's funny," says Walter. "The other day I was on my way home, stopped at a stoplight on Burbank Boulevard, you know—near Vineland?"

On the corner of the intersection he saw a girl standing alone by the curb. She was obviously mentally challenged—Walter used the word "retarded"—large head, those almond eyes and pear-shaped body—she was staring at him. The light changed from red to green. Walter kept his foot on the brake. Waving at the girl to cross the street, Walter held back the line of traffic behind him. They were all honking their horns, but he was stopped, holding them back, and the opposing lane of cars also halted as the girl stepped off the curb, obeying Walter's urging hand. With an ungainly gait, she crossed the busy street safely to the other side.

"Next day," says Walter, "I'm at the same intersection. Burbank and Vineland. Same time of day. There she is again, the same girl, same side of the street. Except that a bus had pulled up, a school bus. I saw her climb on the bus and it took off. It was a bus stop. That's where she waits. Every day. For that bus, y'know—for special kids like her. On that side of the street. And I realized what I had done, the day before."

Walter shakes his head and laughs a little. I zip my briefcase and turn off the desk light.

"You remember that DJ who used to be on the radio all the time?" says Walter. "*Goody Sturdevan*? It was quite few years ago. He used to do drive-time on KPLO—you know, 'Seven seventy seven on your dial!' Arrogant bastard. Just my opinion, you understand. He had these contests. You called in. Seventh caller got seven hundred seventy-seven dollars. But when Goody Sturdevan put you on the air, you had to say 'Goody day!' If you didn't say that, you didn't win."

Walter shakes his head. "I listened to him every morning, but I thought he was arrogant. Just my opinion. But one morning I called and I was the seventh caller. The guy at the radio station who took my call told me not to forget that when Goody Sturdevan put me on the air, I had to say 'Goody day!' Well, screw that arrogant bastard, I was damned if I'd say goody day."

Sure enough, when Walter went on the air, he just said hello.

"'Harumph,' goes Goody Sturdevan. 'What did you say?' I said 'Hello!' 'You sure you want to say that?' I said it again. 'HELLO!'"

Walter looks at the floor. "The first guy from the station gets on the phone and says, 'What the heck did you do?'" He said Sturdevan was furious. I told the guy Sturdevan should drop dead, the arrogant bastard. *What did you say*? He says. I said the bastard should drop dead. And do you know what? Two days after that, I see it in the paper— Goody Sturdevan, radio DJ, dropped dead. Heart attack. I felt a little bad. A little. Well, fuck him anyway. Okay, so, couple of weeks later I look in my mailbox. There's an envelope from Radio 777. Open it up. Seven hundred seventy-seven dollars."

Walter turns to go back to his desk. Then he turns around again. "It's not like I killed the man," he says.

I tell Walter to have a good weekend. On the way home I pass the corner of Burbank and Vineland and look for the girl with the almond eyes but she isn't there. The radio plays softly. I think about someone I used to love a long time ago and it feels like yesterday. The sun is setting over the hills like final judgment in some forgotten language. When the light turns green I step on the gas and drive on.

***

©2018 Rex Weiner

A crime and mystery fiction podcast hosted by two Anthony Award nominated authors

Interviews, book reviews, short fiction & more

Listen in for interviews with: Joe R. Lansdale, Megan Abbott, Laura Lippman,Reed Farrel Coleman, Lou Berney, Meg Gardiner, Ryan Gattis, Sara Paretsky Johnny Shaw and many more!

New episode every month on iTunes, Stitcher & Soundcloud

INDIE RIGHTS

www.indierights.com

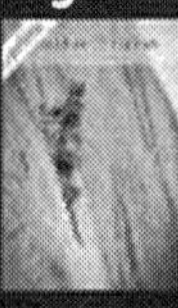

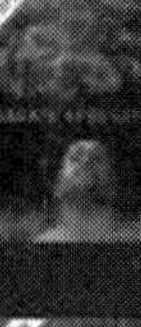

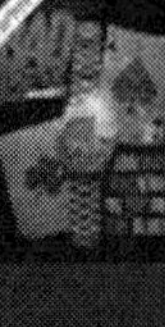

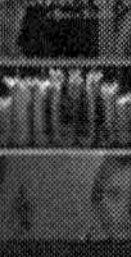

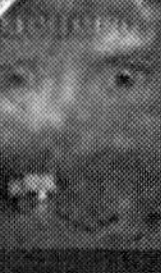
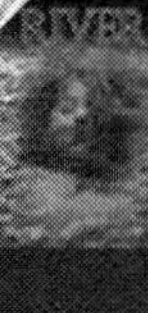

Take a ride with your new buds.

Staunchly Independent Fiction

Pulp Modern
VOL. 2 NO. 3   SUMMER 2018

DISCOVER
TOMORROW'S
BESTSELLING
AUTHORS
TODAY

VENGEANCE

AVARICE

HOMICIDE

All New Stories • No Reprints

Michael Bracken • Thomas Dade • John Kojak
Doug Lane • Chris McGinley • J.A. Prentice
Stephen D. Rogers • Scotch Rutherford • Cynthia Ward

SHARP & DEADLY

DEADLY

SHORT FICTION
SHORT FICTION
SHORT FICTION

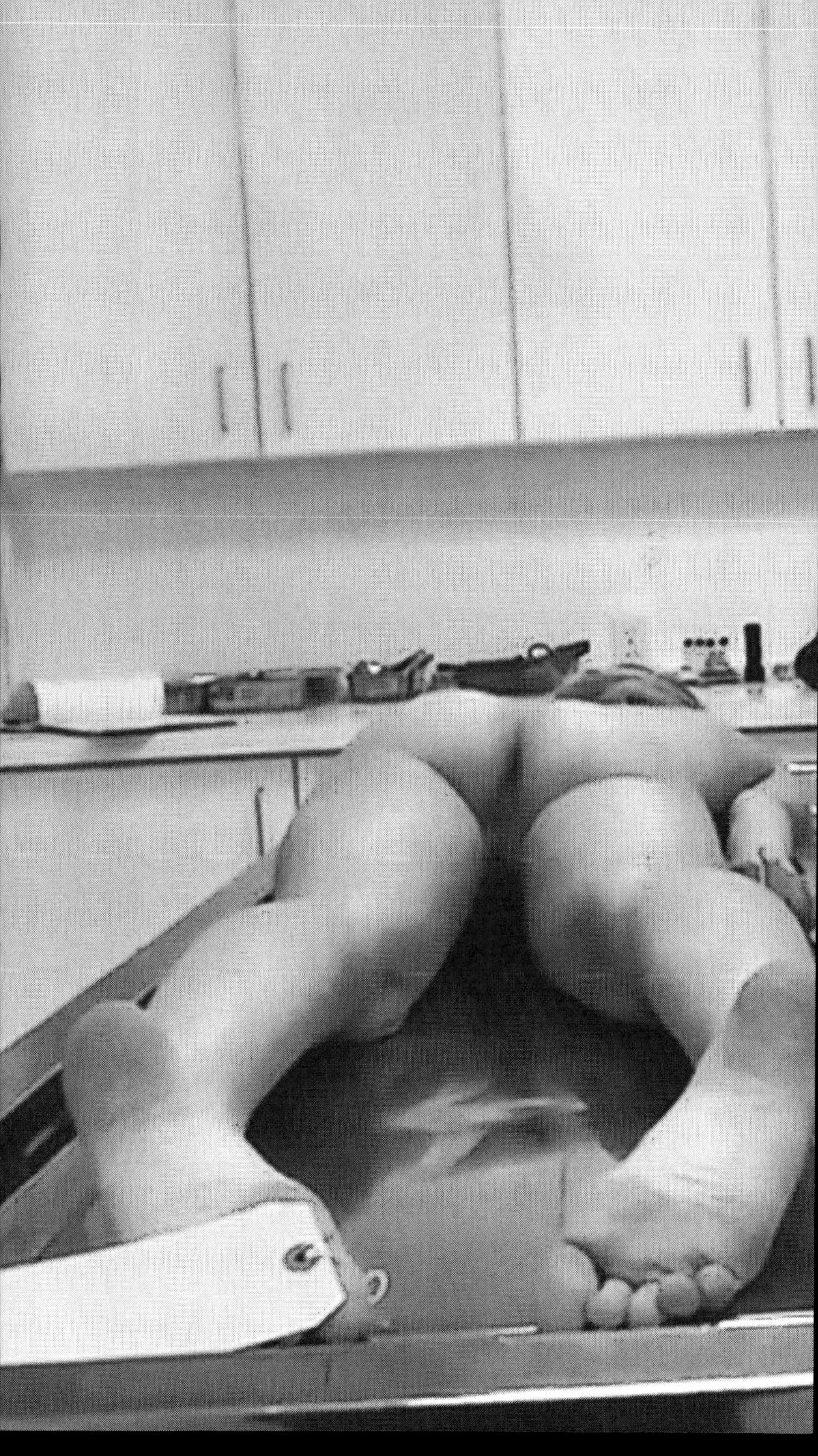

Cold Comfort

By John Bosworth

The first time Ernie's phone rang, he didn't even hear it. He had resolved to teach himself how to cook, and two months into his retirement he had perfected exactly one dish: Beer Can Chicken. He brought his wife, Christine, out to the patio grill to demonstrate the technique.

She was a good sport about it, asking appropriate questions as he used a paper towel to blot moisture from the bird's stippled beige skin. To her, the bedrock of a relationship in its golden years was no different than one in its infancy: an ability to credibly feign interest in the passions of the other person. She bobbed up and down to generate some body heat under her parka, looking like a white buoy floating alone in the dusk.

"That your phone, hon?" she said at one point, but he didn't hear her.

He was absorbed in his work, applying a dry seasoning blend and making sure to touch every cool damp crevice. When the coals were glowing, he gently slid an open beer can into the body cavity and set the whole bird upright on the grate.

"There we are," he said under his breath. He gazed at it lovingly.

"Jesus, Ernie," she laughed. "You haven't looked at me that way in years."

He laughed too, and they went inside where he washed his hands and opened a bottle of wine.

They both jumped a little in their seats when his phone began vibrating on the countertop.

"Is that the timer already?" she said absently.

He gave her hand a squeeze and glanced at the number on the screen.

His heart hiccupped, and then raced to catch up.

"Ern?" she said, looking at him, concerned.

"It's just work," he said, remembering as he did that he no longer worked anywhere. "Something must be up," he added, "I better take it."

Ernie motioned for her to sit and ducked into what had been his home office, now a de facto storage closet. He stood rigidly in a small vestibule created by stacked boxes of holiday decorations. It was cold and dark, but he was sweating.

"You know who this is?" the voice on the other end said.

"Yes," Ernie whispered.

"I have somebody who'd like to meet you," he said. "Somebody like you described."

"I can't believe it's really happening."

"Believe it. Tonight's the night."

"Tonight?" Ernie said. "I'm just sitting down to dinner with my wife."

There was a silence on the other end.

"I'm making chicken," Ernie said, and instantly regretted it.

"It's gotta be tonight. She's on her way out of town."

"What about tomorrow morning?" Did these things ever happen in the morning? Ernie wasn't sure.

"She'll be on a plane to Tennessee by then. Gotta be tonight."

Ernie didn't know what to say.

"Look, don't worry about it," the man said. "I get it. This is last minute. There will be other opportunities. I'll be in touch."

"Wait," Ernie said. He swallowed. "You're in Greenville?"

"That's right."

"It would take me a little while to get out there."

"I know. I'll tell you what. I'm texting you an address. I'll be there from nine til ten, sitting at the end of the bar by the kitchen."

"Will she be there with you?"

The man laughed. "No. You'll meet me there and give me my fee up front. Then I'll drive you to her."

"I don't know about this. Giving you the money first, I mean. How do I know you'll make good on your half of the bargain? It's not like I can call the cops on you."

"I guess you'll have to trust me. Worst case scenario, you have a lovely drive through the countryside. It's fall. Enjoy the foliage."

"That's all the assurance I get for two grand? Foliage?" Ernie snorted. "That's cold comfort."

"Hey, Ernie? That's kind of your style, isn't it? Nine PM. At the end of the bar."

The man hung up.

*

On the highway, Ernie set the cruise control for exactly sixty. Still, he found himself checking the rearview mirror every few seconds. What was he looking for exactly? Police? You're being ridiculous, he told himself, you haven't even done anything yet.

Yet.

The word echoed in his head. He signaled, checked his mirrors, and merged into the right lane. Then he nudged the speed down to fifty-eight.

Even so, traffic was light and Ernie pulled up to the given address, an *Appleby's* sharing a parking lot in a strip mall, at a quarter past nine. He walked to the entrance with his back hunched from the drive, feeling like there was a spotlight on him. He caught a glimpse of himself in the glass of the door and was relieved by the image he saw looking back: a thickset man in later middle age in a golf shirt and khakis. A perfectly normal looking guy.

The man was sitting where he said he would be, drinking a light beer from a glass and watching a football game on a muted TV. He was in his early thirties and quite short, looking a little too small for his jeans and tan Harrington jacket. He looked washed-out. Pale skin, very light brown hair, almost white at the tips, and gold-rimmed glasses. At first glance Ernie thought it couldn't possibly be the man he was supposed to meet. But as he approached the bar, the man glanced at him and then nodded his head toward the open stool beside him.

Ernie took it and ordered a beer.

"Do you want to see a menu?" the bartender said.

Ernie glanced at the man next to him. He looked straight ahead, watching the game, ignoring them.
"I don't know," Ernie said. "No."

The bartender set his drink and a laminated bar menu in front of him, and then disappeared into the kitchen. Ernie and the man were alone.

"That's good," the man said. "Just watch the TV. Keep looking straight ahead."

After a few minutes of silence, Ernie began to feel he had missed an important instruction.

"What did you tell your wife?" the man said at last.

"Work emergency," Ernie said. "Have you heard of *Balthazar's*? On second avenue?"

"Nope."

"It's a specialty wine store. They sell rare bottles retail and online, and, well, it doesn't much matter, does it? I ended up doing some tax work for them last year. I'm a CPA. Or I was. Now I'm retired."

"Congratulations."

"Thanks. Anyway, I told her I had to come back to sign off on some of the numbers."

"On a Sunday night?"

"I said they have to close the books before the fiscal year ends tomorrow morning." Ernie chuckled. "She didn't ask why a fiscal year would be ending in the middle of September."

"Well, she wouldn't have any reason to question it, would she? There's just something about accountants. You assume they're--"

"Trustworthy?"

"I was going to say boring."

"Oh," Ernie said. "Well, I'm not an accountant anymore."

"I stand corrected," the man said. "And what a way to turn over a new leaf. Did you bring the money?"

Ernie looked around, confirming they were still alone.
"Yes."

They both drank from their beers.

"And?"

"Yes?"

"Can I have it?"

"Oh. Right."

Ernie tugged at his pocket for the folded envelope.

"It's mostly hundreds, I hope that's OK. You didn't specify."

"That's fine. No offense, but I have to count it. I don't extend lines of credit to anyone, and certainly not to first-timers."

The man slid the envelope into his lap and riffled the bills quickly with one hand. Apparently satisfied, he pocketed the money and placed a small, cheap looking digital camera on the bar.

"OK, your turn. You turn that on and she'll be the first picture to come up on the screen. If everything looks good to you, then it's on."

Ernie picked up the camera. His shaking hands bungled his first attempt at holding down the power button. He took a steadying breath and got it on the second try. The picture was of a middle-aged woman with dark brown hair accented by a few grays at the temples. She had a round face, smallish nose, and full lips parted over straight white teeth. She stared just outside and above the picture's frame, as if bored or distracted by something. She was naked down to where the picture ended at her navel.

"What's wrong? That's what you wanted, right? You can scroll through, look at some of my other girls if you want. I got a redhead on my string right now. She's a little heavy, but she's alright. Or an Asian, if you're into that. Chinese, I think."

"No," Ernie said softly.

"Or maybe you're into guys? I got guys, too. Just say the word."

"No."

"So what's the problem?"

"No problem," Ernie said, looking down at the screen. "It's just...She's just perfect, that's all."

"Whatever you say, buddy. I try not to get too attached. It's a high turnover business."

Ernie turned to him.

"You don't look like I thought you would," he said. "Like a...you know."

"Like a pimp? What were you expecting? Big hat with a feather in it? An ivory cane?"

"I don't know what I was expecting, really. I guess I spent most of my time picturing her instead."

"Well, maybe I'll take your money," he patted his jacket pocket, "and go buy myself a big fur coat and a leisure suit. That way you'll be able to spot me next time."

Ernie shook his head. "Oh, I don't think there'll be a next time. This is kind of a one-off deal for me. A bucket list sort of thing."

"Ah. 'Once a philosopher, twice a pervert,' right?"

"What?"

"Nothing. It's a quote."

"Well, what's so funny then?"

"Oh, only that I have heard 'there won't be a next time' once or twice before. Usually from guys who become my most loyal clients." He stood. "Let's not kill any more time here. I imagine you have someplace you'd rather be. And someone else you'd rather be with. You'll ride with me to her place."

"You're not going to be there when we..."

"No, no, nothing like that. But I'll be close by just in case." He started towards the door. "Just wait til you get a load of my car. It's not exactly a big purple Cadillac."

It was a plain white full-sized GMC van, a few years old but in reasonably good condition. Aside from its size, it was fairly unremarkable except for a couple of dents in the fender and some lettering painted near the back that Ernie couldn't read, but could hazard a guess at. They rode for a couple of miles on surface streets while Ernie sat quietly in the passenger seat, looking down at the camera in his hands.

When he looked up they were parked in front of a large brick building with a cross gable roof. The man was grinning at him.

"Alright, buddy, this is it. The cat house. The girls are all in there. You ready?"

"Yes. No. Wait a minute. Can I just take a minute?" Ernie was feeling a little breathless. _Breathless with anticipation_, he thought. He'd never understood the phrase until now. His mouth was dry, too, and tasted bad to him. He wished he had a mint.

"I've never done anything like this before."

"So you said."

"No, I mean I've never really done _anything_ before. At all. Nothing, you know, illegal."

The man drummed his fingers on the steering wheel.

"Listen, you're all paid up, take all the time you need. But just let me remind you that we have a fairly tight window we're working in here."

"I know, I know. It's just that now that it's actually about to happen, I feel like such a…"

"A pervert? Creep? Loser?"

"Well…yes."

"Listen, you would not believe how many times I've had this exact same conversation in this exact same parking lot, usually with first-timers. And, Ernie? In the end?"

"…Yeah?"

"Every John goes inside after all. Every. Single. Time. And not one has ever come out with a complaint."

"That's what I am, huh? A John." Ernie did not feel convinced. He felt nervous, and a little ill.

"Look at it this way. You're participating in a time-honored tradition. What's widely acknowledged to be the oldest profession in the world?"

"Maybe farming?"

"Goddamnit, no. Hooking. The pages of history are littered with men who also happened to be Johns. And not just any men. Great men."

"Yeah?"

The man took the envelope out of his pocket and pulled a bill from it.

"See this fella? Ben Franklin? Great guy, right?"

"Sure. He wrote the constitution."

"And the Declaration of Independence, and about a dozen other things, including <u>Poor Richard's Almanac</u>. And believe me, his Richard wouldn't have been quite so poor if he'd stayed out of the brothels."

"Really?"

"Hand to God. A total hound."

"I didn't know that."

"They tend to leave it out of textbooks. Look, the fee technically only covers an hour, but I'll give you til midnight as a first-timer bonus. Sound good?"

"Oh, okay. I mean, I guess so. How long does it normally take?"

"Not too long, I guess. Depends on if you want to talk to her first. You ready to go meet her?"

Ernie nodded. "I guess I'd better be."

"I don't think you'll run into anybody in there, but here." He handed him a lightweight nylon jacket. "Wear this just in case. If you see a janitor or anything, just ignore him and walk by like you got somewhere important you need to be."

Ernie stepped out of the van and zipped up the jacket. It was a size too small for him and his belly poked out under the waistband, but he caught his reflection in the glass of the windshield and he thought it looked pretty good. It was a dark navy material with an official seal stitched onto the left breast pocket in royal yellow thread. Block capital lettering under the insignia matched the three words he could now see stenciled on the rear of the van: County Medical Examiner.

The man pulled a keyring from the cup holder in the dashboard and tossed it to Ernie through the open window.

"Use that electronic keycard on the side entrance."

Ernie looked at the badge. It had a grainy picture of the man printed on it. His name was Dr. Mark Harron.

"Then head down to the basement and take your last left at the end of the hall to get into the cooler. You use the big silver key on that door. She's in drawer thirteen. Do not open any of the other drawers. Do not touch any of the equipment. And hey, most important, whatever you do, do <u>not</u> forget—" he fixed him with a sharp look.

Ernie looked pale, frightened. "Yes?"

"Enjoy yourself!"

He laughed and started the van.

*

At a quarter past midnight, Harron was back, standing outside the door of the morgue. He'd expected to find Ernie waiting in the parking lot, but whatever.

He'd never found a client <u>in flagrante</u> before, but he still offered a polite shave-and-a-haircut knock and waited a moment. When he got no response, he opened the door and looked around.

Well. This was a new one.

He blew a bubble with his gum.

"Oh, Ernie," he said after a minute. "I just knew you were going to be trouble."

Ernie didn't respond, and he hadn't really expected him to. Harron walked over to the table for a closer look. He made a perfunctory attempt to find a pulse and, failing to, went briskly to work.

He wheeled a gurney in from the hallway and aligned it parallel with the table. He hitched up Ernie's khakis, tucked in his shirt, and rolled him gently onto it.

Harron talked while he worked. He told Ernie that carrying extra weight around the midsection, what was known as an "apple" body type, is usually a good predictor of heart disease. He told him that a lot of people make the mistake of thinking they'll exercise after retirement, only to find their bodies were already worn out by then. He told him that, hey, silver lining, if you ignored the particulars of it, Ernie had gone out exactly the way a lot of men claimed they would like to go if given a choice in the matter.

Harron often talked to his patients. He didn't expect any response, but he had worked hard to develop his bedside

28

manner in medical school and enjoyed flexing the muscle. He certainly didn't want to be out of practice should a better opportunity present itself, maybe as a G.P. in a small town somewhere.

He turned his attention to the woman in drawer thirteen, and was relieved to find Ernie's unrestrained weight hadn't had much cosmetic effect. He imagined a grieving family peering into a polished casket somewhere in the middle of Tennessee. "The flowers are lovely but, well, I don't remember Aunty Jane's nose looking quite so...so <u>flat</u>, do you?" Harron chuckled as he scrubbed away all evidence of Ernie's visit. He told her she looked great, very healthy for her age. Which, not uncommon for stroke victims, was true.

He locked drawer thirteen, scrubbed down the table, and got a fresh bag for Ernie. He zipped it up as far as his chin, and then paused.

Ernie, he thought, really wasn't in such terrible shape after all. Just a little heavy. He had a full head of sandy hair, broad shoulders, a big, strong jaw and a dimpled chin. In fact, Harron thought, he had a regular in Akron who had been waiting for an older, fair-haired father-type with roughly Ernie's dimensions for almost a year.

He positioned Ernie as flatteringly as he could under the fluorescent lighting and snapped a picture on his camera. He texted the man In Akron, telling him to call when he woke up, it was his lucky day.

It took him a minute to remember the name of the wine store Ernie had mentioned. Something long and ridiculous. Balthazar's! He brought up a map on his phone. It shared an alleyway with a fabric store and a cafe. There's probably a nice Ernie-sized gap by the dumpsters, Harron thought.

Sure, it would be safer to dump him in the woods. Or rig some weights to him and drive him to a culvert outside the county. But he had liked Ernie well enough, and he didn't want his wife to worry when he didn't come home. Ernie's cover story was pretty thin, he thought, but his experience with grieving families told him she would choose to believe it anyway. A noble death in the line of duty. That might be cold comfort to a new widow, but hey, he thought, that was kind of Ernie's style, wasn't it?

Besides, if Ernie wasn't found quickly, and in reasonably good condition, he wasn't worth much to him.

It was almost two by the time Harron was done cleaning. It would be three by the time he was done in the alley and got home to bed. The cafe opened at four, and he expected to be called to the scene soon after.

The only M.E. in the county was on-call around the clock by rule, but he didn't mind too much. The overtime pay didn't chip away at his med school loans as much as his side business did, but it didn't exactly hurt either.

He zipped the bag the rest of the way up, rolled the gurney to the elevator, and pushed the button. Standing in the half-darkness, he had a sudden vision of himself the way Ernie had thought he'd look. Big gold rings and tailored velvet and maybe even a cape. He had to laugh. The things some people would do to turn a dollar.

***

©2018 John Bosworth

Poling
DRUGS
LIQUOR
FREE
CUSTOMER
PARKING
IN REAR

The Vice Aisle

Mike Payne

If the manager of a *ShopRite* supermarket can be an enigma, Bo Harvey, who'd been managing a *ShopRite* for thirty-five years, was an enigma. Bo perplexed everyone with his refusal to retire. He didn't continue working because he loved the job (as some assumed), nor because he was an empty nester who needed the job's social comforts (he didn't). The reason the poor schlub kept punching the timeclock:

a) He had a lovechild to support

b) His wild double life depended on tips from night shift employees

The lovechild was a byproduct of this double life.

For going on three years, Bo had assigned himself two nightshifts a month. The dayshift employees, as well as the district manager, opined that this proved Bo didn't put himself above the lowly night crew. Bo *didn't* put himself above the night crew, but it had nothing to do with being a team player. The nightshifters' maleficence had given him a new lease on life.

At first, Bo scheduled himself for intermittent night shifts to get away from his wife. He'd married at twenty-one (the same age he started at *ShopRite*), and after thirty-five years, he'd heard every story she had at least 1,470 times and every gripe she had about him at least 14,700 times. Watching forklifts spin and beep into the wee hours was preferable to hearing them again.

On one of his first nightshifts, he crossed paths with the unofficial slogan of nightshifters: "I know a guy."

"You know where I can get some weed?"
"I know a guy."
"You know where I can find a poker game?"
"I know a guy."
"Are there any prostitutes in this area?"
"I know a guy who knows a girl."

Working in a down-and-going suburb just outside Philadelphia, such delicacies were within a tattooed arm's reach.

The best part: people who worked nightshifts were usually the kind that could only hold a job for five or six months (ex-cons, drug users, Peter Pan-types), so they weren't around long enough to brew strong gossip. Once Bo acclimated to this parallel universe, there was no turning back.

His first transgression had been a voyage to a swingers' club. After overhearing two nightshifters discussing "that place in Harrisburg," he had to experience it for himself. "That place" was a huge sex shop with a storage area that became a "disco" once a month, complete with disco-era mores. One could enter for a mere $75.

His first visit was a bust. The mix of people at the disco consisted of two troll-spawned women surrounded by 12 men with sniper's eyes. The disappointed Bo retreated quickly, wondering if the troll-women were plants designed to increase blow-up doll sales.

For his second "disco" trip, he went with a fellow nightshifter named Craig. Craig was a recovering painkiller slave who took a nightjob after graduating from rehab. Withdrawal had caused him so much insomnia he'd never readjusted to daytime hours.

This time the ratio of men to women was more favorable. Bo, who'd been with only one woman prior to his wife, entwined himself with a certified nymphomaniac named Elle.

Elle lived in Hershey, and like Bo, was married. Once a week, the two met somewhere between Hershey and Philadelphia (sometimes a rest stop, where they'd settle for the back of Elle's comprehensively dented van). She brought with her many a side benefit. With her on his arm, Bo could get into any sex/swinger party he could locate (many didn't allow men to enter without bringing a woman). She had appetites beyond sex, which led Bo into another corner familiar to nightshifters: narcotics.

Though Bo hadn't even puffed a joint before working the nightshift, he was soon an informed purchaser of marijuana and ecstasy. Marijuana was easy; four out of five nightshifters smoked it, often in the *ShopRite* parking lot. For ecstasy, he relied mostly on Craig.

His fellow swingers craved more than just sex, and before long, Bo was supplying them with drugs. Within a year of completing his first nightshift, he'd gone from grocery lifer and married celibate to swinging drug dealer. He was working only two nightshifts a month, but as far as his wife knew, he was working five or six. If she had suspicions, she never voiced them.

Life being what it is, Bo's nightshift bliss hit some snags. The first snag: Elle's husband found a marijuana baggie she'd left on the kitchen table. Their marriage had been a sputtering lemon for nearly a decade, and Elle's confessing to pot use convinced her husband it was time to hit the bid on a divorce. Suddenly Elle didn't have to sneak around, which made her demand a helluva lot more of Bo. Her possessiveness and drug-swelled paranoia made their trysts feel less like audits than hookups.

The second snag: Elle got pregnant. Neither of them thought it probable - she was 43 - but there it was.

Bo tried upping his drug selling to cover the child support payments, but with Elle occupied with their daughter, she wasn't available for the swing party circuit, limiting Bo's sphere of customers. His *ShopRite* salary couldn't satisfy his baby bills, and with the drug money dwindling, he had four options:
a) Tell his wife the truth and ask her to get a job to assist with the bills
b) Option a, followed by immediate self-immolation

c) Get a second job, even though he was fifty-six and already working more than fifty hours a week

d) Find some easy work through his night shift network

A former nightshifter named Luis put him in contact with some "low-level guys" who needed a reliable place to do "unsanctioned" business. Soon, the low-level guys were conducting transactions behind the *ShopRite*. Occasionally, they chucked bags in the dumpster. Bo prayed those bags contained inorganic matter.

The payout from these "low-level guys" was decent, enabling Bo to treat himself to a prostitute or two a month. As far as he was concerned, the universe was just again.

One afternoon, Mario the district manager dropped by Bo's store. Mario was almost a parody of the squirrely "yes man," the kind of shill who spent more time at grocery store seminars (enlightening symposiums like *Produce Sections in the Social Media Age* and *Making Dairy Inclusive*) than in grocery stores. To top it off, he had the elocution of a hare-lipped man eating peanut butter.

Mario informed Bo that they were about to become the first Pennsylvania store to experiment with robot shelf-stockers, and what better place for experiments than the nightshift. Once the robots were up and running, the nightshift would shrink to two employees and an IT professional who'd maintain the bots.

A thinned nightshift didn't serve Bo in the least. It jeopardized his vices and secret income, and he could hardly picture the new IT person abiding the black market activities behind the store. The low-level guys would not be pleased.

His mind flipped through possible solutions:

a) Could a nightshifter put him in touch with someone who could "hack" the robots so they'd malfunction and sink the project?

b) Could he get the IT person in trouble with the law, perhaps by planting drugs in his car and dropping an anonymous tip to the cops?

The more Bo mulled it over, the more he realized these solutions were surefire busts. The district manager wouldn't stop until the program was in place. To his surprise, the "low-level guys" took the robot news fairly well. Criminal loiterers no longer transacted behind *ShopRite*.

Three weeks later, Bo and Mario attended the inaugural robot nightshift. Praveen, the robot troubleshooter, and two members of the regular crew—Maurice and Ernest—joined them.

Praveen performed a series of demonstrations with the four "Fetch-O" machines. Around 2:00 AM, they took a break. Maurice curtsied out the backdoor for a smoke.

"Okay, everybody stay right where you are! Don't anybody move!"

Three men with guns and ski-masks barged into the warehouse. One was tall, one was short, one was round. The round one had Maurice in an arm lock.

"Everybody on the ground! On the ground!"

Bo, Mario, and Praveen settled on their stomachs. The round bandit kicked out Maurice's legs and added a supplementary shove to ensure he met the cement floor.

"These all the robots?" the round bandit asked.

No one answered.

"Y'all deaf or something? ANSWER ME!"

"That's all of them," Maurice said.

"Good. Now don't move. I don't want to see no one move."

The bandits attempted to lift one of the robots but promptly gave up.

"Man, how heavy are these things? How we gonna get them in the van?"

The tall bandit barked at the night shifters, "Who knows how to work these?"

The short bandit yanked Praveen off the floor.

"You better get them moving. We need them out of here fast," the short bandit said.

Praveen whispered, "Where do you need them to go?"

The round bandit spoke up, "How we gonna get the things in the van? They ain't making it down the stairs."

The short bandit responded, "We'll move them through the front. We get them outside, put a ramp down, then we put them in the back of the van. Just need to move the ramp outside first."

The short bandit's voice didn't sit right with Bo.

The short bandit continued, "The ramps are heavy, dude, trust me. Should be one in that corner. I can move it with the forklift."

The tall bandit ordered the round bandit to park the van in front of the store. The round bandit headed out the backdoor.

"You get the ramp," the tall bandit told the short bandit. "I'll bring everybody up front with us. All right, stand up!"

Bo, Mario, and Maurice got to their feet. The short bandit zoomed past in the forklift.

The tall bandit said, "Everybody play follow the robot. I'll be right behind, so if you try something, I'll put a bullet in your head. Get the robots moving, but not too fast."

Praveen got the bots in motion; the humans followed close behind. As they made their way out of the warehouse and towards the registers, they heard sirens.

"What the—Craig, where you at?!"

Bo knew the short bandit's voice had been familiar.

The tall bandit ran outside, but the van was already screeching away. Police cars were peeling into the parking lot. The tall bandit turned left and dashed out of sight.

Moments later, the short bandit, now revealed as Craig from the nightshift, rushed back into the store. After glancing around in confused terror, he grabbed what was left of Bo's hair and hauled him to his feet.

"Get moving!"

Craig ground his gun into Bo's neck and together they scampered into the warehouse. Bo did his best to keep pace, fearing a misstep might trigger the weapon. It wasn't lost on him that he was a good bit larger than Craig was.

They reached the backdoor. Bo pictured cops waiting on the other side of the door, pistols drawn. Craig opened the door and pushed Bo out onto the stairs. Bo expected bullets, but the back parking lot was still empty. Craig tried to jackal past him; still aggrieved about having his hair pulled, Bo stuck his leg out. Craig's gun went airborne as he tumbled down the stairs. He got up holding his right shoulder. Bo suddenly realized that if they caught Craig, he might try to lighten his sentence by alerting the police to Bo's illegal activities.

"Go, go, go! Leave the gun!" Bo shouted.

Undeterred, Craig chased down his weapon and got it in hand right as the first police car skidded into the back parking lot. Craig took off. The police car broke hard and the cop on the passenger side leaped out and unleashed a pair of bullets. Craig's body jerked like breeze-nibbled straw and hit the blacktop.

As another cop car sped around the corner, Bo threw his hands up. The accumulating cops all brandished their weapons.

"I'm the manager! I'm the manager! Look at my nametag!"

For the first time in Bo's life, he was ecstatic to have a job that involved nametags.

*

When the bandits had initially barged in, Ernest, the fifth nightshifter, had been off in a corner, where he'd hidden and dialed 911.

The round bandit had tried using the van to outmaneuver the police but rammed an oncoming car and booked a flight through the windshield. AAA couldn't do much about that. The tall bandit got away, a testament to his Division I sprinter's legs.

Craig died from his gunshot wounds. Bo breathed many sighs of relief, which made him feel so guilty he almost broke down and told his wife everything. Almost.

He figured Craig orchestrated the ill-executed inside job with an eye towards pawning the robots. He wondered to whom Craig could have sold them. Not even a nightshifter would know someone looking for a robot.

***

©2018 Mike Payne

Dead Men Tell Tales

Jim Thomsen

I liked the kid from the start. That was a first. Most people, upon unlocking the door to their home and finding me inside, would shout. Or scream. Or make those strangled startled sounds that always make me think of jungle birds. And after they let their frightened eyes drift from my face down to the gun in my hand, they'd start in with the crying, the moaning, the bargaining, the babbling, the begging. I couldn't take too much of that and so I usually made it quick. Which I should be doing all the time anyway. And did, for decades.
But, people interest me.

Like that Chigurh guy in that *No Country for Old Men*, I was fascinated by the choices people made, or didn't made, to bring me to their door. That, and nowadays I like to *be* sure, as opposed to the last thirty years, when I just liked to *feel* sure. Feeling and knowing: the difference between twenty-three, when I did my first, and fifty-nine, which I am now. I know other people in my line of work who say that I shouldn't be paying out string like that, that it wasn't professional, that I should just do what I'm being paid to do and put on blinders to the rest. Maybe I was built that way once. But I'm not anymore, not as I get older and find my books badly out of balance and find that I've lost my taste for doing bad things to people who I later learn weren't so bad. Or bad at all.

It's not like I'd ever not done the job anyway.

And yet.

That person never would have believed that I would not make it to sixty. The person I am now? He knows better. Because he's known worse.

*

I was sitting on a cracked plastic Adirondack chair and reading one of the kid's books—*Pressure Drop,* by Peter Abrahams, one of my favorite authors—when I heard heavy footfalls crunching on the gravel outside the garage, then clunking up the stairs. The door opened and the kid walked in. Dropped his keys on a TV tray that apparently served as a front table. Looked right at me. And then the gun. He stood still for three or four seconds. Maybe an eyelid twitched. Maybe not. Maybe it was merely a flicker of midnight shadow.

Then he drew in a breath. And nodded.
"Well. He said he'd see me in hell before paying me a penny to go away," the kid said. There was a jovial note in his voice, strained and thin, but somehow it stuck the landing. "So this is what he meant. Right?" He closed the door behind him. "I know you've got to do what you've got to do, but, would you mind terribly if I took a shit first? I've really, really got to go, and I would really, really prefer not to be found by my mom with a load of crap in my pants, if you can understand that."

I shrugged, though I wanted to smile. I'd already cleared the bathroom, of course, along with the rest of the tiny apartment. No guns in toilet tanks, or taped to the undersides of tables. No window big enough for someone his size to slide through. This wasn't my first rodeo, or even my fifty-first.

"Sure," I said, motioning with the gun.

"Thanks, man," the kid said.

"Door open, though."

"Oh. Of course."

He flushed a few minutes later. "OK if I wash my hands?"

"No need," I said.

"Right," he said, laughing a little as he came into the living room. "Like stepping around a puddle on the way to the gallows. You know that story?"

"Ambrose Bierce," I said. The kid clapped, looking delighted.

"Mind if I sit?" He nodded to the couch, a horror of bright flowers and burnt orange that looked like it had died and gone to hell in 1974. I shrugged. He sat. If he was nervous, I couldn't pick up a tell. He seemed more resigned than anything else. That was a new one on me. Self-possession is so rare, especially among the young. This kid had it in spades. I had the sense that he would have made a hell of a congressman, or chief executive, or a community organizer. *A young white Obama*, I thought. A ridiculous thought. And yet.

"So," the kid said, leaning forward, steepling his fingers, pressing them to his lips, looking every bit like a manager conducting a job interview. "How does this work?"

"What do you mean?" I used the butt of the gun to massage the hollow at the back of my head, where a tension headache was tugging at me like a drape-pull. The celiac plexus block was wearing off.

"I mean, do you just shoot me in the head or heart? Without prelude? Or does he want more? Torture? Video? Me begging and crying? I mean, does he want me to suffer, or does he just want me gone? Does somebody find my body, or do I disappear forever?"

"Who's 'he'?"

"What? You don't know?"

I sighed and set the gun on the table. A test, maybe. "I noticed some bottles of beer in your fridge. You mind if I have one? You too, if you want?"

"You're going to give me time to drink a beer?"

"Why not?" It was after midnight. The little apartment over the garage couldn't be seen from the street. The main house was dark. It hadn't taken much work to discern that whoever lived there was somewhere else. The puddle of oil underneath the shaded spot in the shape of a fifth-wheel trailer smelled fresh. It hadn't taken much longer, going through the tiny space, to learn that the kid was at his sad-ass job at a big-box store and wouldn't be home until late. The paltry pay stubs and the store schedule were in the same desk drawer.

"You're going to take my life without permission, but you're asking me if you can take one of my beers?"

"You got a point there. And yet." I scratched again. "It seems like bad luck to fuck with another man's beer."

He smiled. It opened up his entire face, like sunrise spilling across the side of a mountain. It was a silly image but it was the only one that came to mind. There was something refreshingly uncomplicated about it. And that thought sent off a dark little depth charge in my mind. Why would someone want to say good night to someone like this?

"Sure," he said, "you can have one of my beers."

Neither of us moved.

"You or me?" the kid asked.

"You," I said, and motioned again. No gun.

"Of course," he said with that same strained joviality. "How silly of me."

With my gun on the table, a foot from my hand, I wanted to see if he would try to lull me or gull me. He passed within a foot of me. Reached into the fridge. Took out two bottles. Grabbed an opener and popped both caps. There was no waste in his motions. If he tried to brain me with a bottle on his way back to the couch, I would have given him even-money odds, maybe even a little better, given that I wasn't feeling so hunky-dory at the moment and wished for nothing more than a hot shower and a hotel bed. But he didn't. He wiped the condensation off with a napkin and handed me a bottle of *Negra Modelo*. Not a beer I'd grown up with in South Boston but one that always seemed to be in every bar I ever set foot in from the road. And there had been a lot of road. Entirely too much of it.

He lifted his own bottle in a light salute. "Here's to never repaying my student loans."

"Sure." I lifted my own bottle and we drank in silence for maybe half a minute. Then he sat back on the couch.

"So you really don't know?"

"Who wants you gone?"

"Yeah, him."

"Nope. It's a transaction, not a justification. No narrative necessary."

"Huh." He took a long pull from his bottle, two-fingered, like some biker in a border-town bar. I had the impression he'd been doing it a long time before he'd ever seen a biker movie. "I guess I had the impression that you liked narratives."

"You're a college kid, I'm guessing? So you know about double blinds."

"Yeah." He wiped his mouth with the back of his hand.

"I don't know who hires me, and whoever hires me has no idea who I am. I'm sure I don't have to explain it further."

"Huh." Another pull. He was almost empty already. "I wonder how you get into work like that. I guess I never bothered to look up 'Murder Broker' on Monster.com."

"Same as anything else, I guess. People who know people."

"The luckiest people in the world, right?"

"Sure," I said. "If you think luck really has anything to do with it."

He rubbed the back of his neck with the flat of one hand and then the other. It was the first self-conscious gesture I'd seen him make. "I guess that's the definition of power, isn't it? Being able to pick up the phone and knowing the number of someone who can make your minor irritations disappear."

"I guess so." I stood and pushed back the chair. He shot me a look that was just short of startled but that was all. I admired that. It was too bad. He had that thing I learned about in the army a million years ago: command presence. More than most of my commanding officers, anyway. "You want another beer?"

"Sure," he said, smiling a little. "Help yourself to another if you'd like."

"Nah. But thanks." I made a forked-finger gesture toward my eyes and back out toward his.

"Oh, right. Of course. My abject apologies."

"I'll get this one." I turned my back on him, just to see what if anything he might do, as I reached into the fridge. I popped the top from my keychain and turned to find that the kid hadn't moved so much as a muscle. I'm not fast anymore, but I'm not slow, either. I looked into his eyes and he looked away and I saw that he'd run through it as well.

I handed him the bottle and sat back down.

"So, tell me."

"Tell you what?"

"Who wants you … you know."

"Who wants me dead, you mean? You gotta be able to say it if you're gonna be able to do it, right?" Point, Kid.

"Sure," I said.

"I thought you didn't want to know."

"I said, they don't tell me. Not the same thing."

"You said no narrative necessary."

"Not necessary. And yet." Here I hesitated, and I never hesitate. "You were right. It's not unintriguing, either."

"Oh." He pulled on his beer and gave his shoetops an eye-polishing.

"My father-in-law," he said. "Stop me if you've heard this one before."

"I might have. Give me the Reader's Digest version."

"What does that mean, Reader's Digest?"

"Short, succinct sentences. A minimum of editorializing."

"Sure," he said, and we laughed a little. "Are you sure you're one of the bad guys?"

"Eh." A wave of weariness swept over me, the lights went a little dim behind my eyes, and for a second or two I wondered why there was a gun on my lap. I needed a Dilaudid. I'd forgotten the bottle back in the rental car. Maybe I *was* slow. "Maybe. Maybe not. Pretty sure."

"OK," he said, wiping his mouth. "Here's a story. About a guy from the wrong side of the Seattle tracks. And a girl from the right side of the New York tracks.

Lust, then love. Then marriage. All very much against Daddy's wishes, which for her, I realized only much later, was the point. But of course she was Daddy's little girl, which meant that it all had to be my fault. I tried to get to know him, but got nowhere. He's like Trump: never change the narrative, never apologize. Punch back harder. Is that editorializing? I hope we both know better. "

"Anyway, her mother had died when she was a kid, so she had some money in trust that he couldn't touch, and I know it made him crazy to have something be beyond his control for once. She used a chunk of it to buy us a nice place on West Eighty-First, used a lot of what was left to put me through grad school at Columbia."

"You said wrong side of the tracks," I cut in. "How did you manage college?"

"Scholarships, grants, loans, night job, second night job. A screaming desire to not live in the apartment over my mom's garage, ha ha. Oh, and selling weed. For which I got caught, by the way, in the last year of my master's degree. I managed to pull enough strings through my profs to stay in school, but with my trafficking conviction, I lost most of my financial aid. I got by with a third night job. And never sleeping. And selling weed again. Which is how I met Verna."

"Love is the drug I'm thinking of," I said. Was I his age when that song came out. I couldn't remember. I couldn't remember who that person was.

"Heh. Yeah." He leaned forward, elbows on top of his thighs, palms cupping his chin like he was a child in church. "I'm still strung out on her. Maybe I shouldn't be, but I am."

"Anyway."

"Right. People to shoot, places to go, right." His eyes bored into mine, and damned if I didn't look away before I could catch myself. "Anyway, I didn't know it at the time, but the money was almost gone. She'd really torched through it, with a couple of years of finding herself all over the world before she met me.

Basically Eat-Pray-Loving her way through life. Daddy knew it. So he saw his chance to get her back.

"He saw me as an extended European vacation. An internship at a nonprofit in the south Bronx. A gap year. But she's almost thirty, and vacation time was over. While I was killing the books, she was reconciling with him. Oh, and with her old boyfriend from her days at Dartmouth, who Daddy apparently loves even more than she ever did.

"They fucked. I found out, because I'm not dumb. I lost my shit, because I'm dumb. Maybe I broke some things. She left. I came home—here—to clear my head. Thought it was just for the Thanksgiving-week break, then I'd go back and we'd cry and hug and work it out and have a candlelight and champagne Christmas."

He dragged his palms down his face and let out a long slow breath.

"But?"

"But." He did the palm-rub thing again. "But, just as I was scraping up the money for my return ticket, I got served. Not divorce papers. *Annulment* papers. As in, the-marriage-never-existed papers. Can you believe that? We were married for nearly three years, together for more than four."

"And so."

"And so." He drained the second bottle, set it down, reached as it wobbled over, missed it. Dabbed at the bit that spilled with the napkin, then laughed. "What am I doing?"

"It's OK."

"Yeah." He squeezed the balled-up napkin like a stress ball, shifting it from one fist to the other and back, over and over. "And so. And so I knew this was all his doing. Maybe she would have divorced me, but she would never have pretended that our marriage didn't exist. She can be deceptive, but she's not devious, if that makes any sense. No, this is a Wolf Of Wall Street maneuver. I can see it still: her crying on his shoulder, him saying, 'It's OK. I'll take care of everything. I'll make it all go away, make it seem like a bad dream. Go let Phillippe take you to Biarritz or Cap D'Antibes for the holiday. It'll all be over with by the time you get back.'"

"Phillippe."

"Yeah. I know. I saw a picture of him on her phone. Looks like he stepped off a Mediterranean yacht in a fucking Wham! Video. Here, a guy like that would get his ass kicked from puddle to puddle in the parking lot of the *Shipwreck Tavern* by six deli slicers from *Fred Meyer*."

"Where you work."

"For a guy who doesn't care to know much, you know a lot."

"I needed to know if I needed to wait here all night."

"It was one of my night jobs as an undergrad. The deli department. My old manager is still there, and I sold him weed back in the day, so he liked me OK and offered me my old job back. I said I'd fill in until I figured something out. He gave me a look like, whatever, you're back, and you're back for good, and we both know it, so bullshit us both about it all you want, I know better. Guess I'm going to get to prove him wrong, right?" He laughed, raised the napkin-ball, aimed at a wastebasket about fifteen away, and neatly banked the shot. "Want to hear something funny? I was going to go meet an old high school buddy at the *Shipwreck* after work. Talk to him about selling weed for him again, maybe some coke, maybe some other stuff. Usually these nights end up with me puking and passing out on the floor of his trailer."

"Why didn't you?"

"Couldn't connect with him. I got out of work and into the parking lot and found that my phone was dead. Not the phone, but the service. Which had been paid for by her. I got cut off."

"So what happened when you got the papers?"

"What do you think? I lost my shit. I called her about forty-seven times until she blocked me. Then I called her dad. Took about forty-seven times, but I got through. Told him a, no annulment, and b, even if I were so inclined, he'd have to pay. I was thinking only of a place to live in New York and tuition for my last semester, but, well, I was yelling a lot and I'm not one thousand percent sure that came across and that I wasn't really trying to extort him, but that I was just trying to build the rest of the bridge to my bright and shining future. There was a pause and then he said, 'No, you're just going to disappear,' and he hung up. "I thought he was just saying that he'd hire some nine-thousand-an-hour lawyer to bully me into settling cheap." He let out a long shuddering breath. "That is, until I walked through the door tonight."

We looked at each other.

"Can I ask a favor?" he said.

"A favor."

"Can we do it somewhere other than here? My mom has always been pretty good to me and she deserves better than to find me here. And the fact that a week would pass—which is when she gets back— would make it about nine thousand times worse. None of this is right, but that shit *really* isn't right."

"Can I trust you?" I said.

"Well, no. But yes."

"What does that mean?"

"It means that if I were in your shoes, I'd shoot me right this second and not look back, because the more you string this out, the bigger the risk that I'll run in the dark or kick at your face or something. You're an old fuck, and you look like somebody's slowly draining your oil, but you look like you can still motor a little."

I said nothing, but the thickening pain inside me told me I needed to get this show on the road. "But, then what?" he said. "You'd eventually get me, or someone else like you would. Right?"

"Right."

"And I'm not exactly equipped to live life on the run, man. I'm broke as dick. And if you looked around here, then you know, so is my mom and stepdad. In fact, they're away because they're scouting out property to buy in Bumfuck, New Mexico because they just told me they're selling the house. They can't rent this place out anymore as long as I'm here, and they were getting twelve hundred a month for it. The housing market is just as hot as the rental market, thanks to the tech-bro cockroach infestation, and they're cashing out at the top of the market. Smart move. Good for them. Fuck me.

"So, I've got nothing to build up from and nowhere to go. I'm no tech-bro. And without that PhD, I can't really get the kind of work that I've been working towards for the last decade. I wanted my wife back, but I accept that ship has sailed. So all I want now to is the means to live one more year in New York so I can graduate and move on to a life of taking care of myself. Pocket change for Pops. But even a broke-dick like me knows that rich people don't stay rich by giving away their pocket change unless it gets them their name on the side of a museum and their picture in the Styles section of the *Times*. So …."

"So?"

"So." He stood, shrugged back into his coat, and shoved his hands into his pocket. "I guess I'm thinking, fuck it. Kill me now. I'm fucking tired of fucking thinking about it. I get it. I'm not allowed to get to the top of the mountain. The top of the mountain is for people born at twenty thousand feet. It was foolish to think I could bootstrap my way into anything worth having. And I'm goddamned if I'm going to settle for slicing fucking deli meat at five in the fucking morning at fucking Fred Fucking Meyer for the rest of my fucking life. So the rest of my fucking life might about well be the next five seconds, or five minutes."

"I see."

"And I'm especially fucking tired of saying fucking all the time. I don't want to be that person anymore."

"I see."

"You see. Great."

I wish I didn't.

"Where would you like to go?"

"What a question."

I waited. Rubbed the back of my head some more with the gun butt.

"There's a beach …."

"OK. You drive."

"Seriously?"

"Seriously." I leaned forward. "But first, I have an idea, if you're game."

*

Forty-five minutes later, I stood on the beach and watched little dots of light grow dim and disappear. The last ferry of the night. I reached into my overcoat pocket for my pack of Pall Malls, the ones I wasn't supposed to smoke since my Stage Four diagnosis, to my burner phone. Fuck the time. It's not like he had ever hesitated to call me in the middle of the night.

"Speak," he said.

"It's done."

A pause. A rustle of bedsheets.

"And yet," I added.

"What?"

"A plus-one was invited to the party."

That was our half-assed code for: *Somebody else got involved, and I had no choice. Happens to the best of us, right? Even me, even if we both know I'm no longer the best of me. So I'm going to need to be paid double.*

"Seriously? That's a first for you."

"A first," I said, fishing out a Pall Mall and a lighter, "and a last."

A long pause. "I think the client will go for that."

"I don't care whether he does or doesn't. Make it happen by morning, please."

"You going on vacation?"

I smiled in the dark. "Something like that."

"Anything I need to know about?"

"Nope."

Fifteen minutes after I hung up, I tossed the gun off a deserted public pier and into Puget Sound. Fifteen minutes after that, I had an afternoon flight booked, Seattle to New York. I would have gone sooner, but I was beyond exhausted. Happened a lot these days. It would serve me right if I died in an anonymous hotel bed.

52

It would serve me right. But it wouldn't serve the kid right.

On the drive, I laid it all out. On the long walk, he'd given me all I needed. Addresses, phone numbers, gate codes, routines, license plates, all that. Even a keycard in his wallet, a card he'd lifted from his father-in-law's home office on a wild impulse. It was as if he knew what was coming. Which he did, tonight. After he told me everything, he gave me a long shiver and a sad smile, one that will haunt me till I hop off this mortal coil. Then he turned to face me and closed his eyes.

I'll never tell this to anyone, but the gun hesitated in my hand.

I really didn't want to do it.

And yet.

I am a professional. A bit more than I am a human being. But maybe I could balance those books a bit by this time tomorrow night, in a *Trump Tower* penthouse.

Maybe I'm kidding myself about that.

And yet ….

I liked the kid from the start.

***

©2018 Jim Thomsen

YAWKEY WAY
CITGO
FEDERAL HEATH
TOW ZONE
NO

The Usher

E.F. Sweetman

Thursday September 27, 1984. Game 159 vs.
Baltimore Orioles. The Boston Red Sox were in a run
of mediocre years in the early eighties, and Fenway
Park was anything but friendly. It was dirty, rough, and
none of the games ever sold out. I was an usher, and I
was young-just twenty-two years old. I inherited the
job from my old man after his heart attack. Don't get
the wrong idea, I didn't just waltz into it; I'd been
working at Fenway since I was twelve. I started out
sweeping up trash, selling peanuts, and programs on
school nights and weekends when kids my age were
riding bikes, or at home sleeping.

Back then we ushers dressed like police officers,
except our jackets and hats were red. That was
intentionally done to keep drunks and rowdies in line. I
grew a long handlebar moustache to make myself look
older. Most of us carried mini bats up our sleeves
when the Yankees came to town. I worked the field
box sections behind the visitor dugout. It was a piece
of cake compared to the bleachers. The perk of the job
was the tips for moving fans down after the game was
underway. I could pull in up to fifty bucks a game,
depending on who was playing.

The '84 Red Sox were stuck in the middle of the
division, with no hope of making it to the playoffs, and
the park was practically empty for the last home stand.
I remember it was the start of a dull Thursday night
game when I looked up in the grandstand, and saw my
least favorite type of fans: three guys from my high
school. They were sitting with a bunch of young girls
that I didn't recognize. Mad Dog, GK and Flip, the

jocks with cool nicknames who went on to college and better lives. They were the guys that made a sport of tormenting me, a skinny loser named Larry. Their specialties were head whacks, shoulders hits, and shoves into the girls bathroom for big laughs.

I did my usual thing when I saw an old classmate, which was pretend I didn't see them. But Mad Dog, the ringleader, spotted me gawking and came right down. I automatically cringed up for some kind of hit, but he gave me a big warm handshake, then slipped me ten bucks and asked if I had seven seats closer to the field. The park was empty. They could have sat behind home plate for free, but I took the ten and told him, "Come down after the third."

They came down with four girls at the start of the third inning, and acted like it was great to see their old pal Larry the Fenway usher. I put them in the fourth row, and made a big show of wiping down their seats. At first I thought the girls were awestruck, but after a few minutes, I realized they were just drunk. The guys settled in among them and kept up a steady beer run, but I didn't toss them because they weren't too conspicuous. I was at the top step when Mad came up behind me with a couple of beers, so I had to ask him, "What are you, a girl scout leader now?"

He shook his head and laughed, "Nah, I'm a high school teacher."

"You're a *teacher*? That's a sweet gig."

He shrugged in an aw-shucks kind of way that looked practiced, and said, "It's not like that, I watch out for them. Besides, they're all seniors."

"Christ, either I'm older than I thought, or they're graduating from high school *young*. Do me a favor, keep your eye on GK," I said, "he's been squeezing the thigh of the girl on his right since she sat down."

I could see the girls worshipped them with their boozy stares and shrieky laughter. They all looked pretty cozy by the eighth inning, and stayed to the end of the game. As they made their way out, Mad Dog stopped to shake my hand again.

"Hey, thanks a lot. Great night Larry, good game."

"What game? Ha, only kidding. Have a good night," I said as I flipped up a row of seats.

"You want to meet us after you get out?"

I looked at him thinking, *Here it comes, he's going to shove me over the seats when I say yes, and they'll all laugh like hyenas.* Mad Dog was holding up a girl who couldn't have been older than sixteen, GK was sucking the face off the blonde he was all over during the game, and Flip had his arms wrapped around two cheerleader types. They had a lot on their hands, so I said, "Sure."

I finished quick and made my way over to a dive bar called *The Dugout* on Commonwealth Ave. I found them crammed into the back booth. GK was on top of the blonde, Mad was busy with his girl, and Flip handed me a beer while he made some room next to one of his girls. From that point, my night got a whole lot better. Things ended after two a.m. in the parking lot off Beacon Street where Mad Dog parked his station wagon.

The only fallout of that night came from my boss. He called me in his office before the start of the next game to chew me out for allowing underage girls to drink in my section. The season ended two days later, and I went into my winter job, loading highway sanders at *Boston Sand & Gravel*, believing I had fallen into some kind of one-time fantasy that would never happen again.

Sunday April 14, 1985, Game 5 vs. Chicago White Sox. Mad Dog, GK, and Flip showed up in the second inning with a bunch of new girls looking to move down from the grandstand for another ten bucks. I put on the show of wiping down the seats for the giddy high school girls. The only thing that was different from the last time was I had to give Mad a warning: no beer for the minors. He got a little frosty, and looked at me like I suggested an impropriety that was out of the realm of his existence, but said, "No problem Larry."

My buddies-yes, I considered them my buddies-were complete gentlemen at that game. There was nothing handsy, no nonsense. And the girls, anyone could tell they loved those guys. They all hung on every word, looked where they were told to look, and laughed at everything. They stayed the entire game, and like the last time, Mad Dog invited me to meet them when I was done working. But instead of heading to a bar, they were going to *Brighams* near Copley Square. I decided to pass. Ice cream parties with teenagers weren't my thing. Mad caught the gist of my answer. He smirked and said, "Okay, some other time, Larry."

That was when I got the gist of how things worked. My buddies brought their little girls to fun places. They did fun things, they built trust over time, to the point where the girls let these guys do whatever they wanted. It was weird to me. Mad, GK and Flip could have had any women their own age for a lot less work. I guessed they liked them young.

Wednesday May 15, 1985. Game 32 vs. Seattle Mariners. The Sox were hanging down in fifth place, and the four game winning streak that started the season felt like it never happened. It was a cold, wet night and Fenway was less than half full. There were maybe ten fans in my section because on nights like that, no one wanted to sit out in the open.

Mad Dog came my way in the middle of the second inning. Right away I could tell things weren't right. He had a cut across the bridge of his nose, his face was swollen, and he was angry. He said he bashed his face going for Marty Barrett's foul ball and hit the railing.

"Christ, you should get that looked at. Did you get the ball? I can have it signed for you."

"Nah, I already gave it away. To some Danish girls we're sitting with who will probably lose it by tomorrow. Hey, can we move down now?"

I waited for the ten spot, but he just stared out at the field holding a bloody napkin to the bridge of his nose. I decided I could cut him a break because he looked like he was hurting.

"Sure, how many seats?"

"Six."

"Party after?"

"Nope."

The way he answered made me feel like I was the weirdo who got sixteen year olds drunk for fun. He came back with GK, Flip and the three women from Denmark who were definitely not high school groupies. As soon as I was done wiping down the seats, the women pushed past me to huddle together and talk to each other in their own language. They also bought their own beer. It was obvious these women weren't into baseball, the weather, or my buddies. Mad just watched the game looking pissed off, and kept a napkin to his nose. GK and Flip kept to themselves on the other side of Mad Dog and drank lots of beer. On one of his trips back from a beer run, Flip told me they met the girls at *The Cask and Flagon*. Mad bought them tickets because they had just come to America and wanted to see a baseball game.

They all left before the seventh inning. Nobody thanked me or said goodbye as they filed out. The Sox lost 6-1. It was one of those nights you could hear a fat guy blow his nose in the bleachers. The only good thing about the game was that it ended before ten o'clock.

I made less than twenty bucks in tips, but it was enough to get warm with a few drinks at *The Dugout*. I was surprised to find Mad Dog, GK and Flip tucked in the back booth with the Danish girls. I got the same cold reception as at the game. Before I could say anything, Mad said, "Look Larry, this party isn't for you."

"Hey, I'm just here for a drink. Cold night, I need to warm up," I said, eyeballing the situation. "Didn't know you guys owned the fucking bar."

Mad looked like he was about to tell me off, then he changed his mind.

"Hey, Larry, maybe you can help us out. Any idea where can go? We can't leave them here like this."

I said, "Jesus. Who gets that wasted on the piss-water they serve at the Fenway?"

They looked at each other, but no one said

anything, and I figured they gave those girls something more than watery beer. So I sat down and struck a deal. I had a key to a trailer that *Boston Sand & Gravel* kept on a work site near MIT. If they let me go along, I'd let them in.

It turned out to be a fun night for me and my buddies. I can honestly say it was not fun for the girls from Denmark, but I doubted they would remember anything anyway. When the girls started to come to, they fought and cried, and I knew it was time for me to make my exit. The last I saw of them, Mad Dog, GK and Flip helping them into the backseat of Mad's station wagon on Causeway.

Two weeks later, about an hour before I was due at the park, I got a visit from a Boston Police Department detective. He said he was looking into three missing women from Denmark. He was following a lead that they might have been at Fenway on May 15th for the Mariners game. I almost shit my pants. He showed me photos of prettier, much blonder women than what I remember from that night. I don't know if it was because I was wearing my uniform, or if he was just a shitty cop, but the detective didn't have any more questions when I said I had no recollection of any of them that night.

A few days later, Mad Dog showed up alone and dressed like he just came from church. He sidled up, but before I could tell him to fuck off, he slipped me a twenty which I shoved into my pocket before he could think twice about it.

"That's for the visit from the detective last week, because you and your buddies are never sitting in my section again," I muttered at him.

"I wasn't sure if the police talked to you. So what did you tell them?"

It was not a conversation I wanted overheard, so brought him down the ramp to the pavilion. It was a perfect day for baseball, but Mad was sweating like it was the middle of August. He was shifty and fidgety. He wouldn't look me in the eye, so we stood side-by-side and talked out of the corners of our mouths.

"I gotta know what you told them," he whined.

"What the fuck did you think I would say? I told them I don't remember seeing any girls from Denmark."

"Jesus, thank you. I owe you Larry."

"Cut the shit. Tell me what kind of trouble I'm in if they catch me in that lie."

His demeanor changed once he knew I lied to the cops for them. He rolled his shoulders and straightened out his collar before he faced me. "Don't sweat it, you're not in any trouble, no one is. Just stick with the story that you didn't see us that night." Then he turned away and headed out of the park.

The missing girls from Denmark made the headlines a few days later. Evidently they flew into Boston with plans to hike their way across America. Their families grew worried that something was wrong after a couple of weeks of not hearing anything from them. No postcards, no phone calls, they didn't show up at any of places they were expected. It was a mystery that nobody saw them, they just disappeared. When I think back to that night, I'm not surprised no one remembers them. The detective showed me photos that looked nothing like them. It was raining that night, everyone were wearing heavy raincoats with hoods, or hiding under umbrellas. As for *The Dugout*, it's a dark bar where people go to get shit-faced rather than remember who was there.

Ten years later, *The Charles River Watershed Association* was dredging near the Longfellow Bridge, and pulled a human jaw with enough teeth in it to determine it belonged to one of one of the missing Denmark girls. They dug along the shore and into the river, but never found anything else. The cold case officially went from missing persons to unsolved murder, but the detective never came back to interview me.

When Whitey Bulger disappeared in January 1995, every missing person, every violent death, every unsolved murder was pinned on him, including the

Denmark girls, although there was not one shred of evidence to point his way.

I lost my job at Fenway in 2003 because I was a no-show too many times. It was no big loss for me. New management came in and wanted to make it a family friendly place which felt a little too over the top. Our uniforms changed. They got rid of the uniforms and gave us ushers baseball caps and khakis like your favorite uncle. The deal breaker for me was that new management strongly discouraged accepting tips. I got laid off from *Boston Sand & Gravel* after the Big Dig in 2007. Now I collect disability for a bad back, bad knees, hearing loss, and I live in a room at the Y.

What little I managed to dig up about Mad Dog and GK didn't make me feel like they were any better off than me. Both were divorced, both retired early. I have no idea what became of Flip except that he moved out to the West Coast.

I keep it all under wraps. I have no doubt it changed me. I did things to the Denmark girls that I'm not proud of, but the one thing I am sure of is they were alive and breathing the last time I saw them. I ran into Mad Dog a few years after they found the jaw. I popped into *An Tua Nua* on Beacon Street late one February night, and there he was, all by himself at the bar. He had lost his looks along with most of his hair, and his belly hung over his belt. He saw me walk in, and tried to pretend he didn't know me. I know I looked like shit, but I wasn't buying that I was unrecognizable.

"Hey Mad Dog, long time, no see," I said taking the spot right next to him.

He stared straight ahead for a few minutes, but I wouldn't go away, so he shook his head and said, "I'll buy whatever you're drinking, but I got nothing to say to you, Larry."

He said it like I did something wrong. He said it knowing I didn't rat him out when I had the chance. He said it because he knew he could. Those guys got away with it because they always do, thanks to losers like me.

***

FLASH'S
COCKTAILS

Chowda

Travis Richardson

"Tastes fishy," Ray said.

Before I could respond with a wisecrack like, "Of course, it's chowda, dipshit," my friend splashed face first into his bowl. It seemed that everybody—-families with screaming kids, buds knocking back a few after work, couples who still believed in that myth called love—-stopped talking and turned to look at us.

"Hey, Ray. Cut it out. You're makin' a scene here."

Nothing. So I punched his shoulder, hard. Nothing doing.

"Ray, this ain't funny. Sit the fuck up."

Some guy came over and said something about being a doctor. Not sure exactly because I was having trouble hearing him, kind of like I was underwater or something. I could hear things, but couldn't make out what they were. So this guy pulled Ray upright and I almost laughed. Ray's face was all covered in white soup with chunks of potato and clam. He looked ridiculous, but I couldn't laugh because he was dead. I don't know how to explain it, but I could tell. Ray's soul had left *Henry's Chowda Shack* and was knocking on Hell's gates right about then.

Ended up he was dead before impact. And it turned out both of our chowdas were poisoned. At least that's what the cops believed, although they were waiting for a toxicology report. Seemed both of our chowdas smelled "unusually fishy." I hadn't noticed and fortunately I hadn't eaten any. I didn't have the appetite that Ray had. But then again nobody had an appetite like Ray. Unfortunately not taking a bite and dying made me the first suspect for the knucklehead cops. Lucky me.

See, my childhood friend Ray was a bastard. One of the worst. He owed me money, a couple grand, at least. And I don't roll around in cash, so that's a big deal. But worse, that stupid bastard had impregnated both of my sisters. So I guess you could say I had motive to rid the world of Ray.

But that bastard also owed other people a lot more money. And by *other people* I mean the kind who only break one leg when they're feeling generous. That's the way Ray played his life, fast and loose without thinking of the consequences. Still to this day, I have no idea why I ever stayed friends with him. I've known him for something like twenty years. Ever since second grade when this confident kid moved to Lowell with moppy brown hair and sly eyes. His single mother took a duplex two houses over. When we first met, he must have known he spotted a sucker.

I left the police station around midnight feeling loopy from an interrogation that revolved around the same question, "Why'd ya do it." I had waived my rights to an attorney because the cops told me if I took one they'd know I was the murderer. Supposedly I slipped the poison in his bowl when he was looking the other direction or something. Mine too. Stupid. I confessed to shouting more than once in the presence of others that I was going to kill Ray. But God's honest truth, I would never make my nieces fatherless, even if they had a bastard for a daddy. Our city's finest, as dense as they are, finally bought it. Leaving, I noticed the cops brought in our waiter, Jeff something or other, and few other people from the Shack.

I drove home, but couldn't go inside my dank basement craphole of an apartment. I kept thinking how I had been one bite away from death. One spoonful and I would've been buried next to my asshole father. A wiser man would've been grateful for living and be done with it, but I was wicked pissed. I wanted revenge, not for Ray, but for me. Ray was a bastard and had it coming, but not me. I didn't even want to to eat with him. I was exhausted from doing a day of legitimate work at a moving company. But he begged me to meet him for chowda. Said he needed to talk to me real bad. Of course I caved in. Like always. Fucking idiot.

*

I went to see my youngest sister, Sam. She'd know who Ray owed money to. Broken up by the news, Sam had taken Ambien with some wine and barely made sense after I woke her. Though Ray had other women, he had a soft spot for Sam and they talked often. That's not the case for Jeannie, my middle sister. She'd cut off his balls if he ever set foot in her place.

"Ray wasn't so bad, you know. Not like people say. Sometimes he's alright." Strands of stringy blonde hair hung across Sam's face. She lifted her hand, but didn't seem to have the energy to pull the strands back.

"Sam, Ray was a bastard. And somebody tried to kill me because of him."

"You too? I couldn't lose both of you. No."

She teared up. I brought her close for a hug.

"Don't you die on me too. I... I couldn't take it. I just couldn't," she mumbled into my chest and drifted into a forward standing sleep.

"Sam," I said, shaking her. "Hey. Who did Ray owe money to?"

"Huh? Ray? Money? Uh... lots ah people."

"I know, but I need names. Anybody threatening him recently?"

"Mikey. Mikey O'Toole's been riding his ass... Sent

a creep over here yesterday. Told me to tell Ray, times up. I hate Mikey. Slimy bastard."

"How much?"

"Wha?"

"How much money did Ray owe?"

"Oh, five grand. But with the vig, Ray couldn't keep up payments… it's probably ten now. Jeezus. Ray, rest his soul." Sam crossed her heart. "He wasn't very smart, was he?"

She looked at me with her bloodshot blue eyes wanting me to say something. But what? Confirmation? Contradiction? Calling Ray stupid is like calling asphalt black, it just is.

"No, he wasn't smart. One of the dumbest dumbfucks I've ever known."

Sam stepped away from me.

"Doesn't mean he needed to die."

"I don't know, sis. But it means I didn't need to almost die for his dumbass."

I felt if Ray were to appear right then and there in Sam's apartment, as a ghost or a zombie or whatever, I would so kick his ass up and down the street. I hate that fucking bastard.

Sam sat on a couch with tears trickling down her face. Why women loved that moron, I'll never understand. Even though I grew up with two sisters, I've never understood women. Seconds later, Sam faded into sleep. I tucked a blanket around her. If I was going to face Mikey O'Toole, I'd need something stronger than just my fists. I searched through Sam's closet, fishing through piles of clothes until I found what I knew would be in there: Ray's old snubnose .38. It was stuffed inside one of those stupid furry boots women wear. As an ex-con, Ray couldn't legally own a gun, so he had Sam hold on to it. My sister could go to jail for harboring his unregistered

weapon. Not that that would've bothered Ray. Fucking
bastard. I stuffed the cold steel piece into the back of
my jeans, peeped at my sleeping niece, Katy, and hit
the front door. Sam was snoring, oblivious to the
world.

*

I played baseball with Mikey O'Toole back in high
school. He was a sophomore when I was a senior. He
was just okay, but he played with the heart of a lion.
Diving for balls he couldn't catch, sliding into a base
when he was clearly out, swinging for the fences on
every pitch. At first it was funny, but then we kind of
admired him because he didn't know when to quit. He
had no off button. He might've gone to college or
minors, but his numerous assault charges squashed
those chances. It didn't take much to piss Mikey off.
One stray look at his girl, you might find your mouth
full of his knuckles.
So Mikey changed his life's game plan, bringing that
same intensity to drug distribution, gambling, and
other less-than-legal enterprises. He bought a bar—
Irish of course—and made it his own. Hip-hop
thumped the entire block. Nobody ever complained, at
least not more than once.
    When the bouncer started to frisk me, which I
didn't expect, I panicked and whipped out the
snubnose. He shook and though compliant, the bruiser
couldn't hear me over the blaring noise. He offered me
his wallet, then his car keys.
    "No, take me to Mikey!" I shouted.
    We walked to the back of the bar, the pistol
pressed against the bouncer's kidney. Mikey,
surrounded by women and goons at a corner table,
smiled when he saw me. It looked genuine. Like we
were playing ball again. His smile dropped when he
stared down the barrel of Ray's gun. I really wish it

69

had been longer, a four inch instead of a two inch barrel, or a Glock or something. I usually don't feel inadequate, but I did then. Especially when I had at least five larger guns pointed at me by his goons. But you go with what you've got, right?

Anyway, the hammer was cocked and I had pressure on the trigger. One sneeze and Mikey's brains would coat the wall. I wanted to kill the man who tried to kill me. Besides, if he wanted me dead, it would only be a matter of time. I felt I had nothing to lose.

"Why'd ya try to kill me?"

"What?"

Somebody finally killed the music.

"Why'd ya try to kill me, scumbag?"

"When?"

"Tonight. *Henry's Chowda Shack*. You poisoned Ray's and my chowda."

"Yeah, I heard Ray's dead. But why would I want to kill you? Or why would I until a minute ago?"

He was Popsicle cool. Like he was in control, asking me the questions. Like he was holding a gun to my head. I don't get how he does that. If you saw him on the street you'd think he was a cocky punk with too many tattoos and piercings and way too much money to burn. He wears those slick European shirts with the buttons open and slicks his hair back. You can't respect that. But there I was, holding a gun to his face, and he's waiting for me to answer him.
I cleared my throat.

"You wanted to kill Ray 'cause he owed you money. I guess you were gonna kill me 'cause I was there with him. I don't like that, Mikey. Not one bit." I said that last part with self-righteous anger, but my hand trembled with nerves.
Mikey smiled again. This time it wasn't kind.

"First of all, call me Mike. I haven't been called Mikey in years. Secondly, why would I want to kill Ray? That asshole owes me money. Excuse me, *owed*. And if I were to kill him, it wouldn't be by poisoning. It would be a painful, brutal fuckin' experience. I'd have pieces of him all over the streets so dumbfucks like you would see what happens when you fuck with me. But you'll be finding out about that soon enough."

He was right. Clear as day in this shithole bar. Mikey (fuck him, I ain't changing his name) wouldn't do it that way, but I knew somebody who could and knew *Henry's Chowda Shack*. I felt sucker punched in the gut. Why didn't I think of it first? I eased pressure off the trigger. Mikey's eyes narrowed. I needed to remove myself from the bar in one piece, hoping against all logic that it was a possibility. But it wasn't my choice. Before I could react Mikey slapped the gun and somebody nailed me on the back of the head. The world tilted with an explosion of pain as my vision bled from purple to black.

*

I woke up freezing and sore. Wet too. I smelled like piss, but didn't want to think about it. I could move, though breathing hurt. Bruised ribs at the least, cracked most likely. It didn't take a genius to figure out what they'd done, kicked the shit of me and gave a bonus golden shower. But I was alive which I wasn't expecting. Sitting up, I realized the final insult: no shoes. Barefoot and shivering, I hobbled from the alley behind Mikey's bar littered with broken glass to my rusted '99 Camaro. It now had the added feature of a busted window with more piss on the seat. That fucker. Then I reminded myself that I was still breathing. I needed to be grateful. This was the second time in five hours that I had missed Death's swinging hatchet or whatever-the-hell sharp thing that bastard carries.

*

I drove with freezing February air pouring through the gaping window. My teeth chattered uncontrollably even though I dialed the heat up full bore. No doubt I was minutes away from hypothermia, but I had to make it to my sister's house in Roslindale. We had a matter to settle.

Jeannie was the middle one. The smart one who could've been, except she met Ray. He destroyed her trajectory and left her pregnant. In spite of all that, Jeannie hustled, keeping that extra mouth fed. She waitressed all over town, including *Henry's Chowda Shack*. But she really started raking in money as a chemist. Science was her thing, and in another world without our deadbeat dad and Ray, maybe she'd be at MIT splitting atoms and shit. Instead she learned to separate Dextromethorphan from cough syrup. Although dangerous and illegal, the profits were too big for her to refuse. She expanded into synthetic smack and crank. Her illicit chemistry business paid for her daughter's tuition at *Sacred Heart* Elementary, and much more. Like a fancy house and furniture.

I tried to warm up in the car, letting it idle for a bit, but I couldn't stand sitting around. She was the one I should've started with, but because I knew what I knew I didn't want to go there. Didn't want it to be true. So much that I stuck a gun in Mikey O'Toole's face and almost got my ass killed. There's a fucking psychological brain scramble for you. A rage started boiling inside. The sooner I confronted my sister the better it would be for her. So I walked up the steps and knocked for over a minute before she finally opened the door.

"What the fuck are you doing making all that

racket? Can't you see I live in a respectable neighborhood?"

Her place was better than anywhere me or Sam had ever lived. She always reminded us of that. I barged through.

"Did I say you could come in?"

"You didn't say I couldn't."

She slammed the door. Looking at her in the light, Jeannie seemed bigger than the last time I saw her. The extra-large robe that used to be loose barely fit her.

"Where are your shoes? You smell like a toilet." That was Jeannie, nothing but positive uplifting words. I dropped my weary bones into a suede leather chair. The one she really liked.

"Don't sit there."

"Can it, Jeannie. You heard about Ray?"

She nodded and some of her bitchy anger seeped out her shoulders.

"Does Lynne-Ray know?"

"No. But then she never really knew him. Ray would only show up wanting money. He barely even acknowledged her. Idiot bastard." She snarled her lips. Jeannie hated as hard as dad ever did. Maybe even harder.

"Is she here?"

"Of course she is. Sleeping upstairs. Where else would she be?"

She stood over me, her fists balled up like she was going to give me my second ass kicking of the night.

"Calm the fuck down, sis. I've almost died twice tonight."

"Twice?"

"I guess you know about the first one."

"What are you talking about?"

I held up my hand with my index finger up. "Ray."

Two fingers. "Poison." The third finger went up. "Henry's. You're connected to all three."

"I don't see—"

"You worked at that chowda shack for years 'til you started your advanced chemistry studies."

"Yeah, so."

"You still got your connects there, don't cha? They're slinging your dope while serving chodwa. Am I right?"

She didn't move a muscle, like somebody pushed a pause button. I continued.

"Why did you kill him, sis?"

"I didn't say I did, but I definitely wanted to. The bastard threatened to expose me to the cops if I didn't give him ten Gs. I don't have that much. Mexican Tar is hot now. Not my products. I gotta keep Lynne-Ray at *Sacred Heart*. Can't have her getting the fucked up education we got. She's gotta have a future."

"What good is her future if her ma's in jail?"

She leaned towards me, her eyes concrete hard.

"I ain't going to jail."

I stood up and got into her face, throwing that hard look back.

"You know you almost killed me? It's stupid luck I'm still alive."

Her face grew even harder. Until that moment, I wouldn't have thought that was humanly possible.

"You introduced me to that bastard. I had a future, you know. I was going somewhere. Then Ray started hanging around the house with you. He came on to me. I was shy. Overweight. How could I say no? No boy had ever wanted to touch me before. I couldn't say no. But you should have." She hit me in the chest. It hurt all over. "You were my older brother, you…you fucking asshole."

I tried to say something, but my throat was too dry.

I wanted to shout I didn't know what was going on
between them, but maybe I did. Ray worked his charm
on Jeannie like he did on all the other girls with the
flattery and extra attention. I thought it was for fun.
Nothing serious, just boosting my sister's ego. I didn't
think he would, until he did. Ray was a fucking bastard
and a half.

"With dad gone you were supposed to look out for
me and Sam," Jeannie said, her voice rising. "But you
let Ray fuck us over. Both of us!"

Then she wailed on me with both fists. It hurt like
hell after the beating Mikey gave me, but I took it. I
needed to hurt more.

"Where were you? Why weren't you man enough
to kick Ray's ass? Kill the fucker yourself? He had it
coming—ever since he stole your goddamn Hot
Wheels in elementary. He was rotten, but you brought
that filth into our house."

She let up on the pounding to wipe away tears. It
looked like she'd been holding back a dam's worth of
them. She muttered "Stupid shit," as she swiped a
sleeve across her nose. I didn't know if I should hug
her or run for the door while I was in this temporary
eye of my sister's raging hurricane. Jeannie wasn't like
Sam. She wasn't touchy-feely in the least.
Then those few neurons or whatever occupies my
thick skull finally started putting things together.

"Wait. You wanted me to die too? It wasn't a
mistake that both chowdas were poisoned, was it? All
because I brought Ray over years ago? Really,
Jeannie?"

She looked at the floor, shaking her head. Couldn't
look me in the eye anymore.
"Aw sis, that's mighty fucked up."

The dam finally burst. Jeannie's face, so tight and
hard with years of hate, crumbled. She let out a low

moan that grew into a loud wail. She collapsed to the floor, her entire body quivering with each exhale. I did everything in my power not to kick the shit out of her.

"Mommy?" a voice came from behind me.

Little Lynne-Ray in her rainbow unicorn PJs stood at the banister. She looked paler than a ghost under florescent lights. I wanted to say something comforting to my niece, but words escaped me. What had she heard?

Jeannie whipped around, steeling herself again.

"Go up to your room, Lynne-Ray. Right now."

"Everything okay?"

"I said go up to your room. Now, you little shit."

She ran upstairs. Jeannie delivered the line just like our father would. Even pointed an authoritative index finger. Dead on perfect.

"Proud of yourself? Acting like Dad."

She picked herself up and wiped snot away with her sleeve. "Somebody needs to be a man in this family."

"You're on thin ice, Jeannie, thin ice." My body shook with hatred.

"Oh yeah, why don't you stand up for yourself? For others? Fucking pussy."

I smacked her across the face. The pop from the impact was as loud as a gunshot. I blinked a few times trying to figure out what I'd done. From the floor my sister looked up, smiling as blood trickled from her lower lip.

"Hitting a woman. Who's acting like daddy now?"

"How did you do it? The poison."

"I was here the entire time, shithead. I got witnesses."

Then it came to me. Like I finally found missing pieces to a puzzle and it turned out be one fucking stupid, ugly picture.

"So when Ray came begging for money, you told him no and then you devised a plan for him to meet me at Henry's. Probably tellin' him that I would give him some cash there. Maybe for dessert, or something, am I right?"

"Keep going, Einstein."

"You had the waiter poison both of our chowdas 'cause he slings for you. But…I still can't believe you wanted to kill me. I'm your brother. Your blood. I don't get it."

She looked at me and I swear she had a gleam in her eye, like she'd been waiting to tell me her dark secret for a long time.

"Every time I see you it reminds me of Ray. And when I think of Ray I think about how you didn't protect me. I was just fourteen for chrissake. Where was my big brother? Yes, I wanted both of you dead."

I don't want to admit it, but I teared up. Fuck, what a messed up life we have.

"So what are you going to do now, big brother? Your sister tried to kill you. Ray is dead. You know who the murderer is. Whatcha going to do? You're real good at doin' nothing."

"I don't gotta do nothing. The cops were questioning the Shack staff when I left. It'll be a matter of time before your buddy breaks. I'm sure the dope you paid him with has already been confiscated."

I lumbered to the door. Everything hurt, inside and out.

"That's just like you, turn your back on family." She shouted as I walked out the door.

"Quiet Jeannie, this is a respectable neighborhood."

As I walked down the steps I saw two police cars, lights off, coming up the street. They must have gotten to the server or cook or whoever to talk. I turned back.

The door was shut, but Lynne-Ray was looking out the upstairs window. We stared at each other. It was if she was asking, "What happens next, uncle?"

Dammed if I knew.

***

©2018 Travis Richardson

SWITCHBLADE
Outlaw Culture
switchblademerch.com
SWITCHBLADE
Outlaw Culture

COCKTAILS

Implement of Destruction

Rusty Barnes

Kraj pulled a Remington sawed-off out of the Subaru's trunk. Louis Gay, also known as *The Fag*, owed Tricky Ricky several hundred dollars. Not much money, really, but it was serial behavior that Ricky worried about, and which had forced Ricky to send Kraj over with a brutish-looking shotgun, albeit unloaded.

The shotgun dangling from his hand, Kraj kicked the door of the office in. "Hello, Louis." Since he'd visited last, Louis had picked up an expensive-looking aquarium filled with fish. Kraj even saw a manta ray in the green water.

Louis barely looked up from his paperwork. "Tell Ricky I'll have the rest of the money next week," Louis said, pulling his wallet out and placing five crispy hundred dollar bills onto his blotter.

"All the money means all the money."

"Can you drop that, please? I've known you since you first got off the plane."

"I have a job," Kraj said. "Just as you do."

"You know, your English is too good. You'd do better slumming it. People might get the idea you had a brain behind that enormous fucking brow ridge."

Kraj sat down in the only other chair. He leaned the gun back against his shoulder. "I'm not here to break anything. Yet."

"Ricky will be fine. Call him if you don't believe me. I've known *him* for longer than I've known *you*."

"Yes," Kraj said. 'That's the point Mr. Ricky is trying to make. It's awkward when you owe money you can't pay back. Word gets around."

"I can't help this one," Louis said. "And it's only three hundred dollars. That Mexican prick can handle it."

Without moving, Kraj kicked the computer monitor back into Louis's chest, knocking him backward, levelling the shotgun across his forearm.

"What the fuck?" Louis said, paling under his fake tan. "I thought we were friends."

"I still have my job that pays my bills." Kraj stood up. "I'll give him the message, but if you don't have it after the weekend I'll be back. It will not be a friendly visit."

"Fuck you," Louis said.

Kraj sighed and pulled the Glock from his belt. He pointed it at the aquarium and pressed the trigger. Green water and brightly colored fish spilled out all over the carpet.

"That cost me over a thousand bucks, you asshole."

"Some of that was Ricky's money." Kraj put the gun back in his pants. "Next week, Louis." He turned and went out the door, Louis cursing and throwing things against the wall.

"I hope Cami gives you AIDS!" Louis said.

Outside, he popped the trunk and wrapped the shotgun in a Mexican blanket and put it behind the tool box. It was time to head home. As Kraj guided the Subaru through the sharply angled streets, he thought about what Louis had said about him. You shouldn't have to strongarm your friends, he thought and the AIDS comment was thirty years old now. No one got AIDS anymore. But then he remembered even Charlie Sheen had AIDS. AIDS and Cami in the same sentence bothered him.

He made a turn onto the Clemens Center Parkway and exited in Southport. He'd gotten tired of his one-room apartment in the basement of somebody else's house. He'd made enough money now through collecting interest and what Ricky paid him to have something decent. Cami had cosigned for him, which he was thankful for, and he had become the sole owner of a two-bedroom condo. Half of an entire house. Ornately Victorian, even the fireplace had gaudy loops and pillars on either side, plus French doors that opened on a deck. The yard wasn't much, but it was fenced in. And now he had a dog named Joe to keep him warm on the rare night when Cami didn't stay over, an ornery Pit with a plain brown coat and of all things, a black tongue. Something strange in his DNA, the veterinarian had said. Kraj didn't care. Pulling into his driveway, he could see Joe already with his paws at the window, waiting for him. Life could be good sometimes, he reminded himself.

He collected his mail from the floor and let the dog outside to piss. He'd planned for Greek salad and bourbon tonight, since Cami wouldn't be in until after her night shift ended at midnight, and he didn't have to work the door at Ricky's club. It was just as well. He and Mikael, the man who ran the club, didn't get along. He flicked the TV on to the news. Nothing new under the sun, except the wars in the Middle East. Kraj shuddered. He'd had quite enough of war. Early on after the Croatian War for Independence, he thought he'd have to hire out as a mercenary or 'security consultant,' but he'd made the trip to America instead and had been infinitely better for it.

His phone buzzed and he made the mistake of picking it up without looking to see who it was.

"Kraj, you prick. I need you at the club." Mikael sounded breathless.

"Who blows you off tonight?" Kraj said.

"Mickey. The prick broke his leg on the gym floor," Mikael said. Kraj began to laugh. Mickey trained furiously in mixed martial arts and karate on alternate nights, but no amount of training had reduced his innate clumsiness, and this was another a series of nights Kraj had covered him. "It's not funny."

"I'll be there," Kraj said. He could make a lot of money on tips working the door. Pretty girls get in cheap, he thought. So much for Greek salad. Now he'd be home later than Cami. He pressed her number, told her where he'd gone and why in a voice mail.

Dressing for the club meant a black shirt and a dark blue tie, though his jeans and boots would work just as well. As he dressed, Joe nuzzled his hand. He'd have to take the dog for a good long run tomorrow morning. It'd been too long since he'd hit a gym with any kind of regularity. Any exercise would be good, but running, at his weight, was no fun. He did it for the pain. He liked pain, dishing it out and getting a little back sometimes. It made him human, and less emotional. He slipped brass knuckles into his right hand pocket and the 9MM into his jeans. Ready to move. He cracked his knuckles and looked into the full-length mirror Cami had installed for herself. It would work, for tonight.

*

The line to get in the club stretched into the parking lot, the first time Kraj had ever seen it so long. Before he stopped counting he'd made two hundred dollars in tips. Lots of homeboys coming in to the city from the surrounding hills, hair slicked back and cowboy boots, or trendy boys in leather pants, and the usual suspects in tight jeans and black shirts, muscled up farmboys that came in to smell pussy for the first time in their week. The crowd thinned by midnight and Kraj went back inside for a drink.

"Here you go, big guy," Amber said, handing him a loaded gin & tonic. She looked fine in black jeans and a fringed top, but the silver tooth always threw him off his game.

"Thank you," Kraj said, throwing down a gulp. He hadn't been able to get inside all night. Now that Kenny had relieved him, he could go out back and get off his feet. He pushed through the swinging doors and into the kitchen, then took the private stairs to the office.

He'd barely loosened his shirt when Mikael came through the door to Ricky's office, Louis Gay behind him with a pistol to Mikael's head.

"What the fuck is this?" Kraj said.

"We agreed on three hundred dollars more, Kraj," Louis said. "This rotten fucker says eight hundred."

"I don't make the rules; I don't lend the money. That's between you and Mr. Ricky," Kraj said,

84

spreading his hands in a placating gesture. "I just collect."

"And he knows goddamned well I don't make the rules either," Mikael said, "but I'm the one with a gun to my head."

"Shut up," Louis said.

"Let's call him," Kraj said. "Mr. Ricky will sort it out for you."

"Mr. Ricky my ass. You fucking Eurotrash asshole." Louis nearly spat at him.

"I can't make the decision," Kraj said. "Let's straighten it out."

"Fuck off," Louis said as he pushed the skinny Mikael away. He took the gun down and dug in his pocket. "Eight fucking hundred." Louis slammed the bills on the table. As soon as the bills hit the table, Kraj had him suspended against the wall, his feet inches off the floor.

"If you ever come in here strapped again I will eat your eyeballs," Kraj said, thumping Louis against the thin sheetrock wall.

"Fuck you, *friend*," Louis said. "Your English sucks. You have no skill in the idiomatic."

Kraj sighed and threw a jab, backhand-slapping him across the throat. Anything more would have crushed his trachea. Louis went down gagging.

"Go home and fuck your woman," Kraj said. "And don't borrow money you can't pay back." Louis didn't say anything. He just walked out bent over and coughing.

"You should've broken his fucking jaw for pulling his gun on me," Mikael said. "You're just going to have to do it later on."

"Not tonight," Kraj said. He briefly ran down what had happened earlier in the day, and Mikael shook his head at every opportunity.

"So you're the reason I got a barrel-mark in the back of my head," Mikael said.

Kraj shrugged. The house phone went off like an alarm bell, and Mikael picked it up.

"Your woman's here," Mikael said. Kraj smiled and tucked his shirt back in.

*

Cami must have stopped at her apartment before she came in. She waited for him at the server side of the bar in a short skirt and a shirt that showed off her toned midriff. Amazing, Kraj thought, that she worked for McDonald's. He wondered how many extra value meals her tits sold.

"Hello baby," Kraj said, smiling as Cami folded herself into him. Just then a woman screamed, cutting through the sound system, so it had to be close by.

"Just a sec, honey," Kraj said. Where *was* the woman? He scanned the crowd by the bar. A small crowd gathered near the exit.

"Kraj, you're not on duty, stop," Cami said.

"I have to find Kenny," Kraj said.

"For Christ's sake, why do they pay him?" Cami said.

Kraj pressed a fifty into her hand. "Drink," he said, pushing people aside to get to the door.

*

One of the rednecks had brought out a knife. Kraj caught him at the very apex of his move toward the door, where Kenny had his arms outstretched trying to prevent the redneck's buddies from moving in as well. Kraj grabbed his knife hand and twisted hard, and the redneck's body naturally followed his arm to the floor. Kraj took the knife away and pressed the heel of his shoe on the man's throat."Calm down," Kraj said.

At the door, big Kenny had managed to push the buddies back out the exit. He stood at the door with a collapsible baton preventing their return. Kraj heard the whoop of a siren. The music cut off.

"Kenny, did you call the cops?" Kraj yelled. Kenny shrugged. "Get rid of the baton."

Kraj had a couple violations on him already, so he jogged to Cami. "Time to go," he said.

"I haven't finished my drink," Cami said. Then she belted down the double Bombay in three swallows.

86

"That's my girl," Kraj said, "now come on." They skittered through the swinging doors and out the kitchen entrance. Kraj stowed his 9MM in the locked toolbox. Too late he remembered the sawed-off shotgun behind it. He just couldn't get caught. That would not be easy. He reached behind the tools for the shotgun and tossed it into the nearest garbage bag. He'd have to be back before seven am trash pickup.

The cops arrived in a swirl of sirens, but Kraj and Cami cut through the back lot of the next-door *Applebee's* and took off on Bancroft Street, staying within traffic guidelines.

"Close," Cami said, primping herself in the mirror.

"I'd say so," Kraj said, still keyed up.

"Are you hard?" Cami said, grinning.

"Not yet," Kraj said.

"Give me time," Cami said, sliding her hand onto his thigh.

*

By the time they arrived at his new place, Cami had him panting. Kraj unlocked the door and slammed it shut with his heel. They collapsed on the couch. Already Cami had pulled his shirt off and locked her teeth onto his collarbone. As he reached to unfasten his pants, he felt a cold nose on his bare back. "Shit." Kraj stumbled to his feet and the dog ran ahead of him.

"Come back to me," Cami said. Somehow she'd already gotten naked, legs spread on the couch. Kraj opened the door to Louis holding a .357 at his chest.

"This morning I said we'd talk, Kraj." Louis pushed his glasses up on his nose. "It's too late for that now."

"I didn't loan you money," Kraj said.

"But you're the implement of destruction. Without you, Ricky has no teeth."

"Somebody will replace me," Kraj said.

"Good point. I bet he'll be easier to deal with. Move inside, Kraj. Keep your hands where I can see them." Louis tipped the barrel of the gun toward him.

"Cami—put on clothes," Kraj said. Cami paled, but complied

"Sorry to interrupt," Louis said. "She's a good-looking slut."

"Fuck off," Cami said as she grabbled on the floor for her shorts.

"Watch yourself, Louis," Kraj said.

"I'm not coming near you, Kraj." Louis stepped inside the house.

Cami had found her shirt, but not her shorts.

"Nice bush," Louis said.

"One fucking time more," Kraj said.

"He probably can't even get it up," Cami said.

"Want me to show you?" Louis said.

Kraj breathed in once, deeply, and broke Louis's glasses with the edge of his hand. The gun went off and Cami screamed. Kraj hit Louis again, a right cross to his jaw. Louis dropped the gun and peppered Kraj's midsection with one, two, three hard efforts, but Kraj had the gun now. He held it by the barrel and cracked Louis in the temple. The body thumped nervelessly, and Kraj breathed deeply again. "Fuck."

"What's the matter?" Cami said. "Bust his ass!"

"You're getting used to the lifestyle. Not a good thing," Kraj said. "I can't go killing people every day. I don't know where to hide the bodies."

Louis moaned.

"Here's something he won't forget," Cami said. She dropped to a squat over Louis's head and let go a streamer of piss onto the man's face. Louis gagged and puked in the same motion, and Cami quickly rose. The dog licked Louis's face and walked away disinterested.

"The fuck?" Kraj said.

"I know. I'm just tired of all these fuckheads trying you," Cami said.

"You just—"

"Let's never speak of it again," Cami said. "I don't know why I did it."

Kraj dragged Louis out of the house and into his car, slamming the door on his leg intentionally."No word of this, Louis. Pay up."

The car's engine whined as Louis gunned it backward out of the driveway and down the street. Next door a neighbor's light turned on then off again.

Kraj turned back to the house Cami was nude again, like a picture silhouetted in the doorway. "Now where were we?" she said.

***

FROM THE BEST SELLING NOVEL
PLUG LOVE
A story where the only cost for true love is being unfaithful
MURDA PAIN
JESSICA RYAN
LANCE WHITTINGTON
SINO HARRIS
NUNU THURMAN
A DEREK SCOTT FILM

Lost Girl

Scot Carpenter

"Fuck you."

Wilferd glared at me.

"Not a chance, sweetheart. When we're done you won't be fucking anybody."

He sat in the chair naked with his legs spread, duct tape holding him immobile. His uncircumcised dick reminded me of chicken necks and that in turn reminded me that I'd missed lunch. I pulled my *Spyderco* and flipped it open as I stepped up to him. He continued to glare, no fear in his eyes. I pressed the point of the blade against the base of his penis. He winced and for the first time that day his eyes flickered.

"I don't have time to fuck around. It's all or nothing right now. Where's the girl?"

He shook his head and looked away. I pressed the blade a little harder. "Which do you want to lose first, your dick or your balls?"

"Fuck you."

"Look, dickhead, if you don't tell me where she is right now you're going to bleed out with your dick stuffed up your ass and your balls for a gag."

"Fuck you."

Obviously threats were useless as was a dead and dickless Wilferd. I tipped the chair against the table so I could pull his head back as I picked up the small bottle.

The label read "Carolina Reaper Death Sauce." A former friend gave it to me as a joke and I made the mistake of putting it on scrambled eggs one morning. I held Wilferd's head back as I poured a shot glass worth of the red fire down his nostrils. His eyes went wide before he pissed himself and started screaming. He started choking and gagging so I set the chair upright and pushed his head forward. Oily red snot ran out his nose and he began coughing and wheezing as the fumes hit his lungs.

For a minute I was afraid it was too much and his throat was closing up on him. He finally started breathing and then crying.

"Oh, shit motherfuckering cunt bastard...oh god, make it stop. Make it stop."

My mouth had been on fire for hours after I consumed a fraction of what I'd poured down his nose. Mucus continued to run out of his nose and tears down his cheeks as he moaned and whimpered. I squatted down in front of him.

"I'll make it stop when you tell me where the girl is."

He shook his head. "I can't, I can't."

I stood up and pushed the chair back against the table. "OK, let's try again."

The bottle waving in front of his face made up his mind. "You won't hurt her, will you?"

"No." Of course I had no idea what the people who paid me would do.

"I'll tell you if you make it stop."

"I'll make it stop after you tell me," I said as I pulled his head back. His eyes rolled as the bottle moved toward his nose.

"OK, OK, I'll tell you!"

"Go on."

"She's at one of Jimmy Richmond's rent houses."

Jimmy Richmond was a well-known name in the area. His family had been here for generations as ranchers. Stories of the parties at his house, the frequent late night traffic at his private air field and photos in Las Vegas papers of him carousing with questionable characters all showed him not to be Rotary Club material.

"What address?"

Wilferd hesitated. "I don't know the address."

Heavy sigh. I pulled back his head and let a few drops hit his nostrils. He shook his head violently, sneezed and screamed again as red mucus spewed out his nose.

"The address?"

He told me and that a guard was with her. His

bleary eyes searched mine. "I told you what you wanted. Make it stop. It burns."

I shook my head. "Sorry, Wilferd. I can't make it stop. It'll go away by tomorrow, though. If I were you, I'd get a *Neti Pot* and rinse my nasal passages with a mild saline solution."

"You motherfucker!"

"You're a fucking mess. There's a sink and paper towels in the next room. Clean yourself up and get out of here."

I cut him loose and watched him shuffle off. What a loser.

*

The day before yesterday I'd walked out to my car to find an envelope under the windshield wiper. It was cream colored with my name written in elegant cursive. It contained a single sheet of paper, a photo and ten crisp C-notes. The attractive young blond woman in the photo smiled widely, showing perfect teeth. On the back was the name Lenka. On the paper were two sentences in the same handwriting:

Find her. Wilferd knows where she is.

I didn't know who Wilferd was but because his parents didn't name him John it didn't take long to find him. After he talked I wasn't sure of my next step. I'd found where the girl is but it wasn't clear what I was supposed to do.

Despite the image of Wilferd in the chair my appetite had returned. I headed to *Dot and Dori's* where I plowed through a platter of chicken-fried steak and fries, adding another layer of grease to my arteries.

Business cards for *New Continental Investigation* didn't have an address because I couldn't afford commercial office space after my partner and I split up. It had been an ugly parting between Suzy and me. Once she found out that I was fucking her brother she said she couldn't stand to be on the same planet with me. That turned out to be false but by the time I realized it, she'd cleaned out the office and the business accounts. I thought that her brother being a cross dresser was at least a partial excuse but she pointed out that he was 17, to which I replied that is the age of consent in this state. That didn't help my case. I don't know if it was his age or the fact that she was pregnant with my baby that made her so vindictive. In any case my financial recovery was glacial. I finished my meal and went back to my studio apartment.

The next morning there was another envelope under the wiper blade. This one had only the sheet of paper with the words:

Where is she? and a telephone number.

A female recording answered the phone. It had a slight Slavic accent and told me I was to be at my usual seat at *Trencher's* at seven that evening.

My Maker's Mark was half gone by seven-fifteen when I saw a woman in a black dress walk in. She sat down next to me. Tall, maybe five-eight and slender, aquiline features. Her jet-black hair was pulled behind her neck. I couldn't tell her age in the dim light. She ignored me while she signaled to the bartender and ordered a double top shelf single malt straight up. She finished it in two swallows and finally looked at me.

She was in her mid-to-late thirties. Her skin glowed milk pale and her gray eyes were like a hung-over winter morning, cold and pitiless. They looked through me rather than at me. "Where is she?"

"Pleased to meet you, too," I said, taking a sip of my drink.

Her face showed no expression as she asked again, "Where is she?"

I sighed and passed her a business card with the information on the back.

She said, "So Wilferd did know where she is, after all," reached into her purse and pulled out an envelope of the same cream stationery. She laid it on the bar in front of me and walked out. There was no note, just another ten Benjamins. I was glad Wilferd had the information she needed. Now that I knew how effective the hot sauce is, I'd have hated to use it all for nothing.

Jerry the bartender came over and said, "Your lady

friend said to put her *MacCallan* on your tab."

"Of course she did," I replied and laid one of the bills on the bar.

The next day the envelope had been slid under my front door. I waited until I got to my morning office to open it. This time there was five thousand and the words "Get her."

As I drank my coffee I considered the letter. The order was certainly open-ended but I'd come to expect that. Exactly how to accomplish it was a question I hadn't an answer to. It was a five-cup problem and as I stood at the urinal a plan began to form.

Sometimes the old and obvious ways were the best. I drove over to the local big box and wandered to the electronics section. My friend TV Teddy saw me and smiled.

"You sign up people for cable here, right?" I asked him.

"Sure. The company installs and maintains them but I get a cut for everybody I sign up."

"Do you know any installers who might want some extra money?"

"Who doesn't want extra money? What's it for?"

I hoped my story made sense. "I'm working a divorce and need to get a bug into the wayward husband's house. So I need the use of a cable installer's van and a uniform for a day. That'll give me access to his system and it'll be easy to hide the bug. I checked and they don't do service calls on Sunday, all the trucks are parked in their lot."

Teddy thought for a minute. "I do know one guy who likes to gamble. He owes money all over. I can give you his number."

I called Harold Owens, told him Teddy gave me his number and that I had a weekend off-the-books installation job if he was interested. We met at Trencher's and he didn't walk out when I explained the deal. He seemed very interested at the prospect of $500. Perhaps the black eye and swollen lip had something to do with it.

For my money I'd get the combination to the gate

lock, a uniform shirt and a set of keys to his van. Sunday afternoon found me outside the rent house. I knocked and a muscular man wearing a *Led Zeppelin* tee and Levis opened the door.

"I've a service request here from Lenka. Says problem with reception."

He said, "She hasn't said anything about it. Let me check."

"Hang on, her system needs a software upgrade even if the reception problem is OK. It'll save me another trip. I'd really appreciate it."

He stared at me long enough to make most people uncomfortable but I smiled and held his eye. He finally walked back into the house saying, "The TV is in the living room" and then continued down the hall.

I heard him calling Lenka. She walked out from the back of the house by herself. Not quite as tall as Gray Eyes but better built, she wore black Capri pants and a white sweater. "Charley say something wrong with TV" in a thick Slavic accent. "I not watch it today. Nothing wrong last time I watch."

She picked up the remote and powered up the system. I gestured for the remote and hit the setup button. She lost interest, went to a wet bar and began fixing herself a drink. I turned off the TV and walked over to her.

I said quietly, "Lenka, the lady with black hair and gray eyes sent me to get you."

I didn't expect her to drop the glass and back away from me, fear obvious in her expression. "How you find me? How you know my name?" She looked toward the hall the big guy had walked down.

"Whoa, wait a minute. I thought you wanted to leave."

She shook her head, "I hiding from lady. She want to hurt me."

"Why does she want to hurt you? I'm only here because I thought you were a prisoner. She paid me to find you and get you."

At that she turned and headed for the hall yelling, "Charley! Come quick!"

Shit, shit, shit. I'd figured to wing it handling the guard but things had gone south way too quickly. Simple plans for complicated situations were rarely a good idea.

Charley arrived all too soon. He didn't have a weapon. I suppose he didn't figure he'd need one. He didn't bother to ask any questions.

He stepped past Lenka and smiled at me. "I'm going to fuck you up." He raised open hands and bounced around.

I put my fists up in a boxing position and shuffled toward him. Let him think I didn't know how to fight. His smile turned into a grin and I wondered what kind of martial art he knew. He'd probably try something fancy to impress Lenka.

A spinning wheel kick is certainly impressive and I was ready for it when he set up. He wasn't as fast as he needed to be so I stepped inside and stopped his leg with my left hand to his ankle then wrapped my right arm around his leg at the knee. I leaned forward, twisted and put him on his face. Kicking him in the balls produced a groan and the twist to his knee would have him limping for a while.

I should have let him up but the look on his face pissed me off. I put my foot on the inside of his knee and twisted his leg again, harder. He yelled, then the yell turned into a scream when I twisted his ankle the other way and bent his leg down to the side. I finally twisted it back as hard as I could. There was a satisfying pop in his knee and his leg bent at an unnatural angle. I twisted it back and forth just to see how loudly he could scream.

"Stop it!" Lenka yelled. "For God sake stop it!"

I stopped, turned to her and said, "Get me a lamp cord."

After considerable effort she brought me the cord. I hog-tied Charley's arms and good leg, then dragged him to a back bedroom and shut the door.

Lenka sat on a leather couch in the living room. She looked up at me with more resignation than fright.

"Are you going to hurt me?"

After that I know he'll help me."

Hearing that made me think I might get a BJ or more out of this, also. It was clear that she's an operator. It was also clear that Nina had expected Jimmy to dispose of a problem rather than fall for it. He must be keeping her on ice until he could work something out with Nina.

Obviously my turning Lenka over to Nina would be finito for both of us. And spoiling any chance Charley had for the NFL or Wilferd had as a sommelier made a friendship with Jimmy Richmond unlikely even if I returned Lenka in pristine condition.

Peeking through the living room window revealed a grey Taurus two doors down across the street that wasn't there when I arrived. A figure was in the driver's seat. I sat down on the couch next to Lenka.

"There's a car down the street that is probably Nina. I'm going to drive around the block and see if it is. You need to stay here. Please don't run and for God's sake don't untie Charley or I'll have to kill him. If it is Nina I'm going to bring her here. Don't panic, I have a gun. I'm coming back whether or not it's Nina. Do you understand?"

She nodded. I gathered up the installer's tool bag and clipboard, opened the door and went to the van with my head down, then made the block and pulled up behind the Taurus. I walked up to the driver's side window with my pistol held out of view.

It was Nina. She'd been watching me in the mirror and lowered the window as I walked up.

I said, "She's inside. I've taken care of the guard."

"We'll go together."

She opened the door and grabbed a purse lying on the passenger seat with her right hand as she stepped out. I didn't give her a chance to get both feet on the pavement but grabbed her left arm and pulled her out of the car, turning and slamming her against the rear fender. The purse went flying. I twisted her left arm behind her and pressed the barrel of the pistol against her kidney, then whispered in her ear.

"That's not my dick. We're going to walk into the

house together just like you said. First you're going to pick up the purse."

Purse in her right hand, her left in mine, we marched to the house. I told her to open the door and we stepped inside. Lenka was standing in the hallway, ready to run out the back.

"It's OK," I said. "I've got a gun in her back."

Nina squirmed so I hit her in the side of the head with the gun. She crumpled to the floor. I pulled up her skirt to see if she had a hideout. No gun and no panties either but a thick black bush I could get lost in for days. I started getting hard as I stared.

"What are you doing?" Lenka demanded.

"Looking for a hideout gun."

"Well, it not in her pussy"

I reluctantly pulled her skirt down and turned to Lenka. "I just appreciate all aspects of women."

She laughed. "You just like women for suck and fuck. I know your kind of man."

I ignored her. My mind was on my problems: what to do with Lenka, Nina and Charley. What to do about Wilferd and Jimmy Richmond.

Wilferd was not a problem because he wouldn't tell Jimmy what he did. Jimmy wouldn't be a problem if he couldn't connect me to any of the three in the house. I doubted if he knew I existed. So all I had to do was deal with three people who were under my control.

I considered options and thought of scenarios but kept coming back to one I didn't like. It was the only one that had a chance of working. I looked at Lenka and smiled.

"Everything's going to be fine. But I'll need your help. You can call Jimmy. When he get's here I'll explain that Charley attacked me and I was just defending myself. When he finds out that Nina wanted me to kidnap you, he'll be glad to get her and realize I've been trying to help you. OK?"

She looked doubtful. "Jimmy get mad very easy. But I'll tell him you helped me."

"That should do it. I've got to take care of a few things first and untie Charley."

She said, "OK" and settled back in the couch. I walked over and turned on the TV then handed her the remote. She settled on a rerun of Dallas.

After making sure Nina was still out I opened her purse and found a two inch .38 revolver. I stuck it in my pocket and then found rubber gloves in the kitchen, put them on, took the gun out of my pocket and walked into the living room.

Lenka was absorbed in the program. "Hey, Lenka" I said and shot her in the head when she turned toward me. She settled into the couch, her head thrown back against the wall. I picked up Nina and carried her back to where Charley was tied and held her upright against me about six feet from Charley, put her gun in her hand with her finger on the trigger and wrapped mine around hers.

"What the fuck?" Charley said just before I shot him twice in his bad knee and once in the side of his head. Then I shifted Nina to the side, put the muzzle of the .38 against her head where I'd hit her, fired and let her crumple on the floor, gun in her hand. Luckily I'd avoided any blood spatter on me.

I hadn't touched much and made sure to wipe it all down, then vacuumed the living room carpet to get rid of the scuffmarks from the fight. Standing by the front door I mentally walked through the scene and couldn't think of anything I'd missed. The medical examiner was an old drunk and the only thing the cops were interested in was clearing cases. It was an obvious murder-suicide and any evidence led back to Jimmy Richmond. I figured he was well enough connected that the investigation would end there.

As Hannibal Smith used to say, "I love it when a plan comes together." Seven grand for 5 days work and I deserved every penny. Looking at Lenka's blue eyes and sagging mouth, the only thing I regretted was missing that blowjob.

***

©2018 Scot Carpenter

103

AN ANTHOLOGY OF NOIR
SWITCHBLADE
TIKI
ADULT
THEATER
XXX
24 Hrs OPEN
PARKING IN REAR
ISS
FIVE

THE
Bunghole
Please
Have Your
ID Ready
GREAT BREWERS
ROGUE
ALLAGASH
Fisherman's
IPA
GREAT BREWERS
MAGIC HAT

Road Rage

Danny Sophabmisay

Hannah rattled in her '89 Spectrum with the air on full. The heat outside pissed her the hell off, and it didn't help that traffic had come to a complete stop on I-94. Bumpers scraped. Horns blared. The potholed road looked like a zoo with all different kinds of animals trapped behind steel and glass cages.

"Sonofabitch," she said. "These fuckin' assholes need to learn how to drive."

Clenching the steering wheel, she rocked back and forth in her uneven bucket seat as the exposed coil springs pinched her ass. Hannah could feel her crooked teeth grinding on each other until the enamel wore down. All she wanted was a hit of crack – just one little rock to unwind after a long shift at The Foamy Beaver. Crack and cartoons would provide her with an escape from the everyday bullshit and put her at the height of human experience. For months, she'd been maintaining a rush until she found out about the baby: Hannah had taken a back alley roll of the hepatitis dice and ended up pregnant by her boyfriend who practiced hitting her for his amateur cage fights. She had to give up and let go of her habit, get clean.

It boiled her over with rage.

Two yuppies arguing in the car next to her amplified her frustration and she started to gnaw on her fingernails. If she weren't knocked up, she'd be sucking on a glass pipe right now. Fuck it. Hannah reached for her cellphone to dial an old plug named Spoon. It was a short drive to his place on Fort Street, and getting high would pass the time until the roads were cleared. She punched in his number and waited for what felt like an hour.

Real mellow, the voice of Spoon came on the line. "Yo, this Spoon."

"Spoon. It's Hannah."

"Hannah. It's been awhile," he said. "If you're lookin' for weed, I got you. Good shit. Fair prices."

"No, I'm not lookin' for weed, man. I'm hopin' to score some rock. Can you do an eight-ball?"

"Yeah, that'd be three hundred."

"Dollars?! That's fuckin' ridiculous!"

"That's 'cause you owe me from last time, and the time before that."

Hannah had always asked Spoon for handouts, and was a little late paying her debts. Without crack, she was messed up, aggravated, and on edge.

"Shit. I need rock, Spoon. What can I do so you'll front me some? Suck your dick?"

"Eh…I'm good. If it were a year ago, yeah, but now you'd have to pay me to stick it between those crusted lips."

"Fuck you," she said, feeling hurt. "Look, I don't have much right now. I will though. Got a job that started last week, and I'll pay you when the check comes."

Spoon let out a bit of a laugh. "You and I both know that's not gonna happen.

Hannah listened to him pulling on a bong and inhaling deep.

"Tell you what," he said. "There's this store across the street from me called Bunghole Liquors. Just go in there and rob the motherfucker. Probably won't be much, but if you get me what you can and throw in an Arizona iced tea, I'll throw you an ounce."

"Come on, man. I'm not about that anymore."

"No?"

"No. I haven't pulled a stickup since April. I'm goin' straight now. I'm pregnant. Can't you just hook me up one last time?"

There was a hard edge in Spoon's voice. "Three bills, or you can clean out the register and get me an iced tea."

Hannah ended the call then chucked her phone down on the floorboard with a hard thud. She continued to sit and shouted at the Cadillac in front of her. Stress had accelerated her heart rate so that it pounded in her chest like a drum. It was as if she had already smoked some crack and the comedown was unbearable. Needles pinpricked her eyeballs. Gunpowder packed her veins. She had been reduced to a state of pure need, itching to rob the liquor store and get to the drug spot.

That's when a Chevy Suburban slammed into her rear end.

Hannah whipped forward like a head banger at a metal concert, and the collision pinned her up against the Cadillac. She let out a muffled grunt, stars dancing across her vision.

"You gotta be fuckin' kiddin' me," she said.

She tried to move around but was pulled back into her mess of a Spectrum. Hannah undid the seatbelt then threw her door open so hard it almost ripped off the hinge. Pushing her on were equal parts hate for the driver behind her and the brutal sun that cooked the hell out of everything. She marched toward the Chevy Suburban as a crowd watched, honking and catcalling.

"Hey, dickhead," she said, pounding on the window. "You think you can just run people over like you own the goddamn road?"

The window lowered revealing a big man in wraparound shades. He had a handsome, smug face that was easy to hate. "You got insurance? From the looks of things, I'd say you don't."

"What's that supposed to mean?"

"It means you either pass me your info, or you get back in your trash-filled car and leave me the fuck alone."

"You're an asshole," Hannah said. She scowled at the man then backed up a step, spitting on the ground.

The big man snapped. "You did NOT just goop on my rims!" He got out of the Suburban and flexed his arms covered in ugly tattoos. "You don't wanna start shit with me."

"Why? Am I supposed to be afraid of you?"

"You should be. I believe in gender equality so I'm not afraid to hit a bitch. I know karate."

"Bring it, Daniel-san! I get hit by my boyfriend all the time."

Hannah clenched her fists as the man closed in on her. Before anyone could throw a punch, a geezer came shuffling out of the Cadillac. He raised his liver-spotted hands in a gesture meant to offer peace.

"Whoa now," the geezer said. "Let's turn things down a notch."

"Fuck off, grandpa," Hannah said. "This shit's between me and him."

"Are we on a playground here? You're both actin' like little brats. It's just a fender bender. I'll call the cops and we can file a report."

"No point doin' that," the big man said. "The only insurance this cunt has is an ass-beating next time I see her." A vein throbbed on his forehead as he stared daggers at Hannah. He waited until she started to turn away. "Yeah, bitch, you better check yourself. Go home to your trailer."

Hannah didn't look back as she returned to her vehicle but saw a group of teenagers piled in a van laughing at her. She was on the verge of tears. Getting in, she watched as all the cars around her still idled in place. She tried not to think about what just happened, and her brain pleaded for drugs to put an end to the madness. Her life had somehow taken a wrong turn and, like the traffic, grinded to a halt. It was all wrong. The assholes. The baby. The addiction. She straightened up and took a few deep breaths before letting out a scream as she pounded on the steering wheel. "Shit! Fuck! Sonofabitch! God fucking dammit!"

Things started to move after that.

Three miles ahead, the police had put up a roadblock but were no longer stopping vehicles. Emergency road flares fizzled out in the blistering heat shimmers around them. Hannah fidgeted in her driver's seat and told herself it'd only be ten more minutes until she could wrap her lips around a scorching glass dick. The need for it was overwhelming.

Coming towards her, a sweaty officer nodded and waved her through.

"Fuckin' finally," she said. "I was startin' to think you boys had nothin' better to do."

Relieved to be moving again, but still irritated as hell, she screeched her tires out of gridlock. The nearest off-ramp curved down into a menacing block of dilapidated homes and businesses, and the now-open road had her wanting to make up for lost time. Hannah stomped on the gas pedal, determined to knock over Bunghole Liquors.

She tuned into a radio station that played the most garbage pop music but was interrupted by a breaking news report on local crime. It was full of static and she couldn't hear much. Sudden vibrations made her jump as she realized her phone was going off. Hannah didn't need to look at the caller ID to know it was her piece of shit boyfriend. He was demanding she get home and give him a blowjob, no doubt. *Come on, babe, I gotta get this tension out before I brawl in The Octagon.* It nagged her something awful, and she cursed herself for selling her Glock 19 with the numbers filed off. What the hell happened to her? What did she do to become so pathetic? Most of all, she wondered what could be done to avoid the all-too-common fate for women in her neighborhood: abused and abandoned.

A low sound soon rumbled in the distance, and Hannah raised her head thinking it was the Channel 4 News chopper that'd been circling the area. She then glanced in her rearview mirror and saw a vehicle speeding around the corner, bass pumping and rubber tearing up asphalt.

It was a Chevy Suburban.

"You again," she said.

The driver was coming up fast from behind and, instead of cutting wide and passing Hannah, decided to wait until the last second to swerve around like a goddamn racecar. He scraped a jagged white line into the side of her Spectrum, causing her to fishtail out of control, jump the curb, and almost mow down a city bench covered in personal injury ads. Hannah shouted as she cranked the wheel back to correct her course. A nuclear combination of anger and adrenaline exploded inside, and what was left of her drug-addled brain told her enough was enough. It had been a long, shitty day, and she wasn't going to stand by anymore and let some caveman push her around.

Hannah was going to run the fucker off the road.

Her beater car groaned as she stabbed her foot down on the accelerator and chased the driver across white lines, down alleyways, and around construction barriers. Oil pumped through her engine like the fiery blood pumping through her heart. She got up on him fast and mean, and she started to laugh. It came out of nowhere and the cackling was uncontrollable. Revenge, she realized, was the one rush better than crack cocaine.

Clouds of red smoke spewed out the back of the Suburban, and Hannah could see that its rear windshield had been splattered in something that looked like paint. She bounced in her seat, hauling ass through an intersection, and followed the SUV down Oakwood Boulevard, where it pulled into an abandoned lot next to a brand-new Dodge Charger.

Hannah threw her car in park, eager to get out and get violent, when she noticed the driver wasn't the same asshole who rammed her in line earlier. His face was hidden behind a Mickey Mouse mask, and he had left the Chevy running hot and was moving towards the muscle car. Slung over his shoulders was a duffel bag stuffed to the point that even a safety pin could rip it wide open, dropping out stacks of cash that were already coming off the top. He yelled at his partners to hurry the fuck up. Donald Duck and Goofy hopped out the back of the smoldering SUV wearing backpacks full of money and gripping M4 machine guns. Everyone was covered in red ink.

"I can't see shit," Donald said.

Goofy dusted himself off. "You shouldn't have been fuckin' around in there, man. Last thing we needed was some bitch slippin' us dye packs."

"I was gettin' into character!"

"You were crowd control," he said, checking his weapon. "Besides, the duck is supposed to be the straight man. I'm the comic relief."

"Tighten up," Mickey said. "The cops are still on our ass!"

"What about Pluto?"

"Fuck him. He's on his own now."

Mickey turned and saw Hannah watching them from across the lot. He didn't hesitate lifting his monster of a weapon and started spraying multiple rounds. Hannah ducked down in her seat as her windshield shattered from the deafening blasts. Glass and dust exploded out. Bullets cut overhead, and she felt her tires pop moments before a hollow point cracked off a huge chunk of her fender. Hannah wanted nothing more than to fight the bastards back. Staying low, she could hear them putting their guns down and jumping in the Charger. She tried opening her door in time but it was jammed tight. Cursing, she climbed over the dashboard and kicked out what was left of her windshield. She tumbled down onto the concrete just as Mickey and friends sped off in a veil of exhaust.

"Goddammit!" she screamed.

Eerie quiet filled the air. Hannah surveyed the scene and assessed the damage. Her Spectrum had dozens of bullet holes spaced out across its frame and was a chewed up hunk of metal. The only thing left intact was a Garfield doll suction-cupped to the rear windshield. She then caught her reflection in a shard of glass and gave a pained sigh. Her eyes were bloodshot and spiteful, and her brittle hair was blown straight back.

"Ain't this a fuckin' mess," she said.

She glanced over and watched some loose dollar bills blow around the lot. Most were stained, unusable, but she thought they'd be good enough for people who sold crack out of abandoned homes and on lonely street corners. The money led up to the Suburban like a trail of breadcrumbs.

Hannah walked over, reached up, and opened the driver side door. Everything was covered in red coloring, and there was a man slumped over in the passenger seat looking like he crapped out after a night of heavy drinking. His Pluto mask was off, resting on top of his head, and he had both hands covering a stomach wound that pumped blood onto the leather interior. Next to him was a gym bag full of hundred dollar banknotes wrapped in plastic.

Hannah hopped in for a closer look, feeling excited in a way she couldn't even understand.

Pluto looked at her and tried to speak. "They...They left me. They fuckin' left me.

"No shit," Hannah said. "That's what happens when you roll with a bunch of assholes."

"You gotta take me to the hospital, lady. I don't care about the cops finding out. Just drop me off at the curb."

"Like hell."

She took a closer look at the bleeding Disney character who turned whiter and whiter with each passing second. Her eyes went back down to the bag of money. It was enough to start over fresh and new.

"I'll pay you half," he said.

Hannah laughed. "You seriously think you're keepin' any of that?"

"Fuck you!"

Pluto made a grab for the .45 sitting in his lap but Hannah stopped him by yanking on his arm. She hit him in the face with her free hand then reached for the pistol and put it up to his temple. Her finger tensed and the trigger got pulled. Gun smoke filled the confined space of the SUV as brain matter exploded out of the man's skull and dripped down the window in gooey chunks. His eyes never closed. It was a sight that made Hannah uncomfortable, so she fired at him again and again and again. The barrel was still smoking as she put the Suburban into drive and peeled out of the abandoned lot.

She didn't know if it was the acceleration or the thrill of driving a stolen vehicle with bank money and a dead body, but she was feeling wild. The freedom was amazing. It reminded her of the good old days when she was knocking over gas stations. If only she'd had a boulder of crack on her right now, it would've made for the perfect moment. *Fuck Spoon and his overpriced bullshit*, Hannah thought. She planned on taking the dealer for all he had and shoving a tall can of Arizona iced tea up his ass.

Hannah was less than a mile away from the drug spot when her run ended. She stiffened up and looked out at the road ahead of her as a fleet of police cruisers surrounded the SUV.

"Get the fuck out of the vehicle!" the cops shouted. "Get out! Now!"

Eyes wide with alarm, Hannah slid her hand down to the floorboard for the comfort of the .45.

A stocky officer with his gun drawn flung her door open. He screamed at her to not move a muscle and to keep her hands where he could see them while another cop came and dragged her out from the SUV. He threw her to the ground, driving his knee into the small of her back as he handcuffed her. There was no point in struggling against it. Hannah just laid there, bathed in red and blue light with her arms restrained. She watched as the stocky officer leaned into the Suburban and retrieved the .45 along with the gym bag full of loot. She stammered about the gun not being hers, about the money being legit, and about how someone must've planted the corpse to frame her. The officer just laughed. Hannah started to laugh too. She knew she was screwed, and that her entire shit-life had been leading up to a moment like this.

"On your feet," the cop said, pulling her up.

Escorted into the back of a squad car, she noticed a long line of vehicles forming on the road. It was a queue of chrome that stretched back as far as the eye could see. Brake lights flared up, and drivers slowed down to watch her getting busted. It made them feel better knowing they weren't in the same predicament: addicted, pregnant, and headed to prison. Hannah couldn't complain though. The cops may have caught her, but at least she wouldn't be caught in the goddamn traffic.

***

THE BARGAIN

Tom Barlow

Tanya King could remember how her father sneered at a neighbor when the man bragged about the deal he got on a Cadillac at the Columbus police auction. If it was a bargain, he said, one of the local used car dealers would have snapped it up.

So it was with some trepidation she bid on the last car of the day, a 2008 Honda Civic Si with a four-speed stick shift and 162,000 miles on it. The few people remaining, mostly Somali, looking for cars Uber would permit them to drive, were apparently put off by a deep dent in the passenger door, rust on the rear right quarter panel, a star burst in the windshield, and bald tires. The only dealer left on the bidding floor told her she was lucky to get it for a grand. Had it not been for the foot of snow that fell overnight there would have been a couple of pirate drag racers looking for a vehicle they could use to scavenge parts. Nonetheless, after she paid the clerk, received the title, arranged insurance and purchased temp plates, she felt a great sense of accomplishment. She'd brewed thousands of lattes to pay for this, the first car she'd ever owned. No more bus for her.

On the way home, she pulled a CD of *Kendrick Lamar's* latest out of her purse, intending to test the in-dash player, but the disc slipped out of her fingers and fell down the gap between the driver's seat and the center console. Cursing, she pulled into the parking lot of an old strip mall before fishing around beneath the seat for the CD. Instead, her fingers encountered something soft, wrapped in plastic, that seemed to be fastened to the bottom of her seat. Curious, she exited the car and knelt beside it so she could get a grasp on what seemed to be a package the size of a box of Velveeta taped to the underside of the seat. She tugged it free, and as soon as it came in view she opened the opaque wrapping to reveal brown powder. Her old nemesis heroin? It was the same color and consistency as the kind from Asia, and what else would be concealed that way? Her heart began to race.

Tanya looked around to make sure she was unobserved before fishing further under her seat. There she found three more bricks of dope, each a pound, easy. She piled them on the passenger seat, removed her jacket and draped it across her find. Her breathing was jagged as she returned to the driver's seat.

Her apartment roommate had moved out earlier in the month, so when she arrived home Tanya was able to smuggle the dope inside unobserved. She placed the bricks on her bed and sat there for half an hour staring at them, fighting as hard as she could against the urge to smoke up just a pinch. Her *Narcotics Anonymous* group would warn her that even the slightest slip could result in a full-fledged return to the addiction she'd fought so hard to overcome, through three relapses before she was able to remain clean. On the other hand, if she could sell it the sudden fortune might allow her to realize her dream, to move to one of the sunshine states and attend modeling school. That was worth a little risk.

If she took that direction, though, she really had to determine if the dope was real. She finally gave in enough to carefully unwrap one so she could scoop up a few grains of the powder with her little fingernail. With tears in her eyes she raised it to her nostril and took a quick huff.

Bang. She thought her head was going to explode at first, then that all too familiar warm, calm euphoria that had suffused her life for five years took over. The stuff must be much purer than that available on the street. When she found herself pondering where she could score a needle she shoved that thought aside and stashed the dope deep in her closet.

Tanya was tempted to think of her find as karma for all of the crap she had endured in the six years since she dropped out of high school. From the first time she had smoked up a balloon of Mexican brown to the first time her then-boyfriend Kyle Bordergard made her earn her way by turning a trick, her life had been chaos. Over time, the brutality and shame wore her down to the point that, when an undercover cop approached her about helping set up a bust, she agreed, as long as they would help her get clean afterward.

*

She sat on the dope for two anxious days. The nights were not so difficult; she'd always felt comfortable in the dark, free of the spotlight that shines on beauty and failure. The days, though, were one long slog of cravings, which she fought by attending NA meetings each day before and after work.

The problem with selling her find was she had rarely bought drugs for herself. Kyle was always the one to score the heroin. Despite the way they parted, he was the only one she knew who might know how to unload her find now. Fortunately, he was greedy, and chronically broke. Could she insinuate herself back into that world without yet another relapse, though? And would he forgive her for putting him in jail, albeit briefly?

If he was true to form, he'd be on the nod shortly after supper, so she waited until 9 p.m. to drive over to the double just east of the Ohio State campus, hoping he still lived there.

There was no doorbell, so she knocked, waited, knocked again, before the door was cracked open by a girl she remembered as a regular at Kyle's parties for the last year before they split. Kyle liked to call her by her full name, Andromeda, but everyone else called her Andi. The girl was even thinner than she remembered, with a streak of lime green in her bangs.

"What you want?" the girl said.

"Hi. Remember me? Tanya?"

The girl licked her front teeth. "Oh. Yeah. You looking for Kyle? Because him and me are together

120

now, so I don't think you're welcome." She didn't open the door further.

"I'm not interested in Kyle," she said, "not in that way. I have some business. He could make a lot of money."

The girl frowned. Her pupils were the size of BBs, the kind of eyes Tanya had seen in the mirror every day for five years.

"Wait here," Andi finally said, and closed the door.

A couple of minutes passed before it was opened again, by Kyle. "What the hell are you doing here?" She opened her purse and turned it toward him, revealing the brick of dope. "I found this and it's got to be worth a ton of money. You help me sell it and I'll split the cash fifty-fifty."

His eyebrows rose and his mouth puckered. "Come on in."

As soon as she entered the living room he shut the door behind her and said, "Strip."

"What do you mean?" Tanya said.

"I mean, take off your clothes. All of them."

"I'm not here to fuck, I'm only here for the money."

"The last time I saw you, you were wearing a wire. So strip. It's not like I haven't seen it before."

Tanya peeled off her coat, sweater, bra, boots, socks, and wiggled out of her jeans. She hadn't bothered with underwear in years. Naked, she spun in place and said, "What's next? A cavity search?"

"You need to eat more," Kyle said. "Your ass is disappearing." He reached into her purse and grabbed the one brick of junk she'd brought. She didn't want him to know she had more until she was sure she could trust him handling the sale. As she dressed, he dropped a pinch on the coffee table in front of Andi. She eagerly dropped her face to the table and snorted it up.

Her eyes rolled up and she trembled for a minute before reaching up and grabbing her hair with both hands. It took another moment before she said, "Day-um. That's strong shit."

Kyle, apparently satisfied, said, "Where'd you come up with it? From the evidence room?"

She explained about the police auction, her find. "I figure the car was confiscated in a drug bust and somebody forgot about the search. You know anybody that would buy it from us?"

"How much is there?" Kyle lifted the brick to gauge its weight.

"Just shy of five hundred grams. And purer than the Mexican shit we always had."

"At $50 a gram, that's what? Twenty-five grand? Figure they step on it four for one before it hits the street, they could pay that much and end up selling it on the street for over a hundred grand."

"So can you get to someone who would buy it for twenty-five grand?" Tanya was good with numbers. "That would be twelve-five each."

"Yeah, I know a guy who knows a guy. Leave it with me." He slipped it under his chair.

"I'm trusting you on this," Tanya said.

"And I'm trusting this isn't a sting this time. You turn on me again, you're dead," Kyle said.

*

Tanya waited a nervous two days, every hour at home a battle with the three bricks in her closet, to hear back from Kyle before he made the news on the TV above the alcove at work. His body, fished headless from the Olentangy River, had been identified by his fingerprints.

Horrified, she was thankful that she hadn't been the one to attempt the sale. She left work with relief at 3 p.m., but her phone rang as she reached her car. Tanya recognized Kyle's cell phone number so she answered with great trepidation.

Andi was crying so hard it took a minute for Tanya to recognize her voice. "They're going to kill me," she said. "They think Kyle had more of their dope."

"Who?" Tanya said. "You want me to call the cops?"

"No cops! I got a gun to my head right now. You got to give them the rest of the dope."

"What dope?"

122

"He says they lost four bricks. He figures if you
have one, you have them all. You got his car, right?"

"Who?"

"He says it's none of your business. You meet him
in the parking lot of the Jack in the Box in an hour with
the rest of the dope or you're a dead woman."

"How much is he willing to pay?" Tanya said.

She could hear someone laughing when Andi
passed along the question.

Before Tanya could ask for clarification there came
a loud clap and the phone on Andi's end rattled as it
fell to the floor.

*

Her first instinct was to get high, stay high, her
second to hit the freeway and head west until Ohio
was a distant memory. But she had to face the reality
that she had no money to fund her flight.
Thankfully, Andi didn't know where she lived. The
apartment was still in her ex-roommate's name, and
she hadn't been in touch with any of her old druggie
friends since she cleaned up, so she could hole up
there for the time being. Her boss at work was kind
enough to grant her a few vacation days when she
called him to explain that her mother had taken ill.

She used the pay phone at the *7-Eleven* down the
street to call the only other person she could think of
who might have some information about the current
drug scene, Pierce St. John. He was an on-again, off-
again addict and artist for whom Tanya had modeled a
number of times in return for dope.

"Hey, Pierce," Tanya said, "This is Tanya. King.
You remember me?"

"Hey, honey. How're things with you? I heard you
kicked."

"I'm clean but could be better. You know they
found Kyle murdered? Word is he was trying to sell a
brick of heroin. You heard anything about that?"

"It's all people want to talk about. Rumor has it that
was Bogdan Dudin, and he's supposedly looking for
some more dope that he lost. You involved in that?"

"Thankfully, no," she said.

"Dudin's warring with Pete Orlov over the heroin market in town. It scared me straight, I'll tell you."

"How do I get hold of this Orlov guy?"

"Are you sure you want to? He's a real gangster."

"At least he didn't kill Kyle. So, yeah."

"It's your life. I know he never misses a game of the Summer League. It's a basketball league for college kids and guys who never went to college but dream of going pro. NBA scouts supposedly drop by sometimes. Orlov's son plays there, at the Stevenson Rec Center, Tuesday nights."

*

Tanya kept the lights off and the drapes pulled in her apartment. Sunday evening was a bowling night for her parents, so she took a risk and drove over to their house while they were gone to steal the 9mm Glock 22 her dad kept in his nightstand. She felt better with its heft in her purse.

Back home, she found it impossible to sit still until she snorted up just a miniscule bit of the dope. She rationed herself thereafter to one pinch every four hours.

Someone began calling her cell phone every half hour from a number she didn't recognize, so she didn't answer the first fifty times. Eventually, though, she snapped.

"Tanya King? About time," the voice on the phone said. It was low and raspy, like a cigar smoker.   "You got something belongs to me, and if you want to live, you'll give it back."

"You must have the wrong number," she said. "This is Debbie Kirkpatrick."

"Bullshit," Dudin said. "I heard your voice when you were talking with Andi."

Tanya hung up, now more terrified than ever. The phone kept ringing, though, day and night.

*

By Tuesday evening, she had screwed up the courage to try to sell the dope herself. After smoking up a tenth of a gram in her car to bolster her courage, she entered the rec center.

124

At the Summer League games, it wasn't hard for her to pick out Pete Orlov. He was surrounding by three of the most intimidating punks, wearing leather jackets although the gym was at least eighty degrees. They locked onto her as soon as she entered, as did most every other man, including the point guard dribbling the ball, who had it stolen. She was so used to the desire in men's gaze that it bothered her very little any more.

Orlov, middle-aged, trim, wore a beautifully cut suit, sky blue with a white shirt and a paisley tie. The girl pressed up against him, quite young with biracial features, scowled at her. She approached them and climbed three steps before telling the body guard closest to her that she'd like to talk with Mr. Orlov. The guard turned to his boss and repeated her request. Orlov nodded. The guard pulled her purse toward him and looked inside. Tanya was glad she'd left her pistol in the car, but the brick of junk caught the man's attention. He raised his eyebrows and tilted the purse so Orlov could see what was inside. The man nodded again and the group parted to allow her to climb up to him. He whispered to the girl sitting next to him, and she rose and climbed the stairs until she was out of earshot. She gave Tanya a venomous stare.

Tanya was growing used to jealous girlfriends.

Orlov patted the bench next to him, smiling. Tanya took a seat.

She introduced herself.

"You related to Ushon King?" he said.

"I don't think there's any Ushon in my family. My people are from Zanesville."

"So what you want with me?"

"I have a problem, and I hear you have one too. I thought maybe we could help each other out."

"Go on." He took her gently by the hand.

"Maybe you heard that Dudin lost three bricks of junk. Well, I've got them and I need cash. I'll sell you the fifteen hundred grams, top quality stuff for $50,000. It'll bring you four times that on the street."

"I don't know how you confused me with somebody who deals drugs, but I'd like to learn. We need to talk somewhere private." He removed his hand, stood, brushed his lapel. "Boys, we're leaving."

His entourage stood as one. "Come on," he said to Tanya.

She followed the group out of the rec center to a stretch limo that was parked in a handicap spot. There, one of the group slipped behind the wheel while the others walked over to a white Lexus SUV with smoked windows.

Orlov opened the back door of the limo and waved her inside. The girl followed her before Orlov entered.

Tanya took a seat with her back to the driver compartment, which was sealed off with a plexiglass window. Orlov and the girl sat facing her.

"First things first," Orlov said. "Please disrobe. I need to make sure you aren't wearing a wire."

"Really?" Tanya said. Getting naked was beginning to be a bore.

"All the way, bitch," the girl said with a cruel grin on her face.

Telling herself that she needed to get used to her skin if she was to succeed in the modeling world, Tanya disrobed. The car had not yet heated up and she was covered in goose bumps. She spun around for Orlov before reaching for her pants.

"Not yet," he said. "Come over here." He patted the seat next to him.

If her dreams were not on the line, she would have walked right then. Instead, she hopped over and sat where he indicated.

He immediately put an arm around her, his hand falling to her breast. "We going to do business together, you need to do me a favor, OK?"

"What favor?"

Orlov nodded to the girl sitting on the other side of him. She reached over, unzipped his pants and fished out his cock, which was already hard.

Orlov took Tanya's hand again and guided it to his cock. "Show me you're not working with the cops by sucking me off."

The girl giggled and leaned over for a better view as Tanya, feeling she had no other choice, lowered her lips. She'd given head before for as little as a fix, so she could do it one more time for fifty grand.

After she was done and dressed, Orlov and his girl snorted up a line each of her heroin and were very pleased with the result. Tanya joined them, just to get the taste out of her mouth.

Once he was satisfied, he tented his fingers and said, "I could just take the dope from you, you know that, right?"

"I only have the one brick with me, and I have a friend knows I'm here, who would call the cops if something happened to me."

He waved his hand as though shooing a fly. "Forget that. I'll buy the prick's dope from you, but first you need to help me take care of a problem."

"What's that?"

"You help me kill Dudin."

"I'm no killer," she said.

"I don't need a killer, I need bait. Next time Dudin calls, you set up a meet at the Steel Wheels Truck Stop out on 42. Leave the rest to me."

They only had to wait ten minutes for her phone to ring again, on the half hour. This time, she answered it, Orlov leaning forward to catch both sides of the conversation.

"You come to your senses yet?" Dudin said to Tanya. "I'm giving you one last chance to walk away from this alive. You make me hunt you down, you won't just die, you'll beg me to let you die."

"I need money to get out of town," Tanya said. "You bring five grand and I'll swap you for the rest of your dope. Then I leave town, you never hear from me again."

"How do I know you aren't setting up a sting? I heard you did that before."

"You'll have to take my word for it. And no, I'm not getting naked to prove it to you. You meet me in the parking lot of the Steel Wheels Truck Stop out at the U.S. 42 exit off I-70 at nine this evening. Bring the money and I'll give you the dope. I'll be in the Honda."

"I don't like it," he said. "I got another place in mind."

"I don't care, I'll be at the truck stop. You can either come or not." With that, she hung up.

*

After hitting the *Barcelona Restaurant* for dinner, Orlov's treat, they launched their plan at 7:00 p.m. While several new men headed off to reconnoiter the truck stop in a black panel van with a plumbing company logo, Orlov in the limo and the rest of his goons in the SUV followed her back to her apartment where she picked up the remaining two bricks of heroin, so they could execute the swap as soon as Dudin was dealt with. They then drove to the truck stop together, Orlov's limo leading her in the Honda, the white Lexus SUV pulling up the rear. Still a bit high, Tanya was tempted to keep the dope and bail, but knew she was only alive by Orlov's indulgence and any escape would be temporary.

The truck stop was an oasis in the January darkness when they arrived, asphalt acres surrounded by frozen corn fields on three sides, U.S. 42 on the fourth. The restaurant at the center was only sparsely populated, while the pumps were almost vacant; the gas station across the freeway was underselling them by a dime a gallon.

On the south side of the center building was a huge lot for truck parking, although there were only a few semis there at the moment. Orlov backed into a space adjacent to the restaurant. From there he could see Tanya park at the far end of the truck lot, fifty yards from the nearest semi, right at the edge of the corn field and at the outer limits of illumination from the yard lights. To her east, she could see the white SUV with Orlov's soldiers parked across the road in the *McDonald's* lot, while to her west the panel van full of

128

men waited by the tire inflation station. She presumed they planned to catch Dudin in a crossfire. She had no trouble envisioning herself caught in the hailstorm of bullets when the war began.

They were absurdly early, and as she waited she was dismayed to realize that some part of her was still fighting the plan to give up the dope, demonstrated by the temptation to snort up a line to calm her nerves. The effort required to ignore that yearning left her with a need to piss. She exited the car, but instead of walking to the restaurant and exposing herself to potential witnesses or gunfire, she chose to make her way into the frozen corn field until she was enveloped by darkness. Just as she dropped her pants, though, a full hour before she was due to meet Dudin, a Cadillac crossed the lot and slid in beside the Honda. As soon as it stopped, a double-trailered semi pulled up behind and crosswise to the two cars and stopped, blocking them from the rest of the truck stop, including Orlov's troops.

Two bulky men exited the Cadillac holding assault rifles and approached the Honda. When they confirmed it was empty, however, they obviously sensed a trap. They quickly returned to the car, waved the truck driver to move aside, and backed up the Cadillac to execute a turn.

However, as soon as the truck exposed the Cadillac to the rest of the parking lot, all three of Orlov's vehicles came screaming across the parking lot to box it in. A fusillade of bullets quickly turned the Cadillac into a pock-marked piece of junk metal. Before Orlov's crew could escape, however, and before Tanya could return to the Honda, a Hummer and a black Buick Firebird appeared from the far reaches of the lot, full of more Dudin soldiers. They stopped thirty yards from Orlov's troops and begin returning fire. As the pitched battle reached a frenzy, the semi that had been blocking the action earlier appeared again. Having circled the restaurant to pick up speed, it plowed directly into the van full of Orlov's

people, shoving it into and on top of the SUV. As
Tanya watched in horror, the car pile caught fire.
With that, the driver of the semi jumped down,
revealing a body bound and gagged on the seat
beside him. He calmly walked to Dudin's Hummer, got
in, and it and the Firebird sped away.
In the roar of the fire, Tanya raced to her car, panicked
and thinking of nothing but escape. But just as she
reached it, the door of the shot-up limo popped open
and Orlov stepped out. Bleeding profusely from a
wound in his neck, he ripped open the passenger door
of Tanya's car, tossed in the bloody plastic bag full of
drug swap money, and made to get in next to her.

Tanya had no time to think, so instead the longing
she had worked so hard to suppress acted for her.
Before Orlov could get in, she pulled the 9 mm from
her purse and shot him twice in the chest.
After he collapsed to the ground, she reached over
and jerked the door shut before she tore off, driving
the periphery of the lot to stay out of the yard lights. As
she entered the freeway, heading west, the old familiar
sense of failure drove her foot down on the
accelerator.

*

By the time the sun dawned behind her
somewhere in central Iowa, Tanya was fiercely high
and fighting two conflicting temptations: to stop in
Omaha long enough to score a needle and a spoon, or
drive across the median to meet a semi head-on.

With three bricks of heroin now back under the
seat and plenty of money to buy more, with her habit
back in full bloom and a murder charge in the offing,
this piece of shit car from the police auction was
proving her father right. It had been no bargain, not
when she totaled up the real cost.

***

©2017 Tom Barlow

130

The Magician's Left Hand

Tais Teng

The Nazis bombed Rotterdam back in World War Two, a regrettable mistake because the Dutch government was at the point of surrendering. The bombs turned all those quaint little alleys and churches into rubble.

The city got a brand-new heart, though, all black skyscraper glass and aluminum. Our very own Dutch Manhattan.

A hundred nationalities walk the streets, their skin color ranging from Frisian pale to Senegal black. Me myself, I'm something in between: Indonesian Dutch, what they call an Indo here. We are getting rare, though. Most people think me a Mocro: a Moroccan, or a Turk. We had lagged behind in the race to fill the Dutch delta with as many babies as you can.

I don't advertise. Word of mouth is enough.

My iPhone chimed the required three times, broke off and started again.

"Meet me at The Nieuwe Blauwe Engel," a man said. He remained just a gruff voice: no face timing there.   "You know the place?"

"I thought they closed. Had to close. The cops."

"They reopened."

"How do I recognize you?"

"You won't need to. I know your face."

I didn't like that much, both The Nieuwe Blauwe Engel and that "I know your face". Meeting in a known underworld haunt is a truly bad idea and my public face is deliberately nondescript.
I took the metro, rolled three billfolds just to keep in practice.

I haven't always been a hit man. I started out a magician, as fast fingered as the best. But I would never be as famous as our own Hans Klok: most of my gigs were children's birthdays or staff parties with drunken employees. "Yeah," they sneered, "show us your rabbit!" Or: "Where is your beautiful assistant?"

Rolling stuff was slightly less boring, but being a pickpocket seemed a step down from a world famous magician. Hit man was a good compromise: I never liked people much and there are too many of them already. Every time I rubbed someone out I heard the Earth sigh with relief.

I got off at the second stop and put the billfolds in a padded envelope. It was already stamped and addressed to the Lost and Found office. Three girlfriends back I had promised Linda that I would never steal again. I can't seem to hold on to girlfriends but I keep my promises.

*

Every balcony had a blank satellite disk turned to the sky. The boys lounging at the corner would scream "Whore!" to every passing girl without a headscarf. It was that kind of block.

The Nieuwe Blauwe Engel had a winged showroom dummy in front, raising a one gallon beer stein.

I never got inside. A woman walked up to me and said: "It is you?"

"I suppose so. It was someone else who phoned me, though."

"Just an app. Changes your voice."

I looked at her. She was beautiful in a hard way, her face all perfect planes and cheekbones to kill for. A generous mouth lipsticked a mat pink and silver filigree earrings. Cafe latte skin. What my youngest brother would have called a high maintenance dame.

I did my automatic inspection: No needle tracks on her bare arms or nicotine stains on her fingers. She was almost aggressively unaddicted. Good. I never work for junkies, no matter how wealthy.

"I know your price," she said, "and I won't haggle."

"Fine. Nobody under sixteen though. Or over eighty. I don't do inheritances."

She studied me for a moment. "I see. Your people, you think that old people are somehow saintly? Wise?" She clacked her tongue. "Some people are born bad

133

and remain that way." She hooked her arm in mine. "Let's walk."

She smelled nice, coconut oil and mimosa. Her skirt reached all the way to the top of her cowboy boots, but her cleavage was deep enough to leave little to the imagination. Full breasts that moved with every step. Her hair was straight, bobbed and tinted a platinum blond. The hair should have warned me. Most girls wear it very long now, with curly hair extensions. I prefer it shorter and platinum blond is my preferred color. She clearly had done her research.

"Where are we going, exactly?" I asked.

"Somewhere without camera's. The new lip-reading apps of the cops are way too good.'

"Hey you, habibi!" a man catcalled. "Dump that Turk and come with me." He made that smacking sound with his lips.

Now "habibi" means something like "sweetheart". It is almost respectable, but that Tssk! Tskk! sound certainly isn't.

She glared at him and he stepped back, raised his hands and shuffled back in his portico. A waft of stale urine reached my nose.

"My friend here," she said, her voice very clear. "He is Maori. He would cut off your head without a thought and eat your tongue."

"I didn't mean anything!" He fumbled with his key and the door clacked shut behind him.
Cut off your head and eat your tongue. That was a new one for me. There is always a hierarchy among criminal newcomers: when I was a teen the former Yugoslavs and the Russian Mafiya were the cold-eyed killers, emptying their Uzis on the police cars that tried to chase them. Perhaps I should get one of those temporary tribal tattoos?

She halted. "Here." She waved at the cameras on the street lanterns. Their lenses had been spray-painted black, I saw. There would also be no video cameras watching from the windows: the dealers didn't like snoopers.

"Well," I said, "who and where? And do I go all the way or just a warning?"

"An ear won't be enough. Or a finger. It would just make her angry."

"Her?"

"And now you suddenly don't do women?"

"It isn't that. I was just surprised. As long as she isn't under sixteen or over eighty"

"She isn't. And all is fair in love and war as they say."

"A rival?" I asked, meaning: Is this love or war?

"The less you know…" She clearly cherished her clichés. She took a picture from her silver bag. "This is her. Lydia Vermeegeren."

Just the face. Long black hair, curling. The mouth was one huge, inviting smile. Silver lips. She almost sparkled. It must be a picture plucked from a dating site.

"She looks a lot like you." Not her hair or her make-up, but I am almost as good as an airport scanner in recognizing the real face underneath, the shape of the ears, the nose, the way the eyes are set in the skull. And the color of her skin was the same. Exactly the same.

"My twin sister. She used that resemblance to rip me. Intercepted a whole shipment. One I had already paid for." Her beautiful lips compressed into a thin line. "Five million euro.'" She shrugged. "Family ties only go so far. I want her dead. The address is on the back."

"I see."

"Will you shoot her?" She sounded strangely eager.

"A knife works without a bang and it gives the cops no bullet to measure. I would have to dump my gun and a knife is much cheaper."

"Heard that about you. The knife in the dark and you never wear a bullet-proof vest."

"A point of professional pride. I want it paid in advance. Not half now and the rest later."

"I know. Give me your account details. Bitcoins it was?"

"Dollars are for amateurs."

The Darknet is fast. No waiting time. The numbers appeared in my shielded account the moment she stopped typing.

Bitcoins are a nice way to move money, but a bit iffy. Any preposterous bubble will pop in the end. I mostly use them to buy the truly valuable stuff. Never gold or diamonds: rare earths like neodymium and terbium. No smartphone works without them and they are getting in short supply.

"She will be at home at nine o'clock," my client said. "She is very reliable that way." She touched my shoulder, walked away.

I followed her with my eyes. Something was wrong, deeply wrong. It must be the way she walked: almost ungainly? Tottering. Wait, her cowboy boots were high-heeled, almost stiletto heeled. She took the big steps of someone who never wears pumps, who prefers to be able to run if needed. She had disguised herself, and changing your footwear to something unfamiliar or too tight is one of the best methods.

*

The times us professionals needed informants in the police corps are long since past. What we need is a good hacker and the Chechen are the best.
Back in The Hague, Ladislav shook his head. The backroom of his brother's bakery looked like a last century's brothel: gilded mirrors, red velvet chairs and several most deplorable lamps that kept changing color.

"Nothing in the databases and that is not only the Netherlands. Interpol en Sûreté, too. No trace of any Lydia Vermeegeren having a criminal record."

"I thought so."

"An alias? I can try to crack it."

"No. We try it the other way around. This picture, scan it."

Ladislav beamed: it was the relief of a professional who can do his single trick after all.

"I got you your Lydia. Is it a problem she has been dead for seven years? And that her name isn't Lydia?"

"No problem at all."

136

Later that afternoon I drove past Lydia's house in a
taxi (never use your own car when stalking your prey!)
All houses were the same, red roof tiles and tiny front
gardens. Like a child's drawing, I thought, and their
lives would be equally identical.

I had my high-speed camera pressed against the
window. I saw the address was right when I inspected
the pictures at the next corner. One showed a small
copper plate with the name L. S. Vermeegeren.

Nine o'clock my client had said. It would be dark by
then.
Killing people is no harder than slaughtering a pig.
Just never see them as human and never ever look
back. Only a romantic fool notches the grip of his colt
after a kill.

There was a full moon just rising above the
rooftops. It was kind of red which seemed appropriate.
I could have come in from the back: magicians and
pickpockets never need a key. But that was probably
just what she expected. No victim ever saw me, or so
the tale went. Just the knife and a shadow moving
away. Never an eyewitness.

I walked down the garden path. The gnome with his
wheel barrow looked brand new: not a trace of algae
or moss. And the copper nameplate still gleamed. It
must be as recent as the garden gnome.

I rang the bell, stood in front of the door. Most of
the houses had a sheet of pebbled glass: this one was
solid oak with a single spy lens. Footsteps, the rattle of
a key and the door opened.

"Yes? What is it?" The question was pure theater:
she held a gun pointed at my heart. It was a small
caliber, a woman's gun, but big enough to kill a man
pointblank, a man moreover who prides himself on
never wearing a bulletproof vest.

She looked exactly like the picture: a wig with long
curling hair. Her footwear, though, were stout walking
shoes, no doubt with steel noses.

"You killed my sister," she said. "It took me seven
years to find her killer." It was a short speech but one
which she must have tried out a thousand times, until

only those two perfect sentences were left. She stepped back, pulled the trigger.

Misdirection is a magician's stock in trade: he waves his right hand while the left stuffs the dove in his pocket. Nothing my clients believe about me is true except for me preferring a knife.
I cut her throat with a single swipe: the sudden drop of blood pressure makes a victim faint immediately while a stab into the heart has to slip exactly between two ribs.

I looked down at her slumped body, the bubbling blood. The picture had no doubt been authentic and she had disguised herself as her twin sister for her revenge.

*

In the car I shrugged out of my bullet-proof vest. Even with a state-of-the-art and very expensive liquid-armor vest, the shot left me with a nastily bruised and possibly broken rib.

I sat for a moment, frowned while I tried to remember that particular victim. Long black hair, silver lips. All that about stealing a shipment was probably true, only it hadn't been from her sister.

Nothing surfaced: there had just been too many victims. And what is the use of a butcher remembering the pet names of his pigs?

***

©2018 Tais Teng

138

Video Arcade

Violet

Evelyn Deshane

When Violet glanced up from her book, all she saw was the woman. In the basement of *Back Door Rentals*, the light was never that great. You had to walk down a set of concrete stairs before getting to the door, half-obscured by darkness. Even inside, the low florescent bulbs above the sections were only there to provide enough illumination to read the titles while also casting safe shadows for customers to hide in.

But the woman seemed to brighten the entire shop. She stood in the middle of two aisles, framed by the doorway, as if she was caught in a living art piece; a reinterpretation of the birth of Venus. In this version, though, the sea-shell that gave birth to beauty was two aisles of VHS pornography, most likely of lesbian and fisting variety.

The woman broke the tableau with a step forward. And Violet recognized her right away.

The woman in the rental shop was the same woman from the first porn movie Violet ever saw. The dark hair, nearly to her waist, appeared as black as it had been on the TV screen. Her pale skin was exactly the same and led up to the same prone throat. Only her smile was different. This time, it was tense and terse as she locked eyes on Violet behind the counter. She held her winter coat around her body tightly, and hunched herself over, in an attempt to keep the men from staring too hard at the living legend who had now graced their store.

"Hello," the woman said. "You work here, yeah?"

Violet nodded. She didn't want to speak in case her voice cracked and gave away her deeper testosterone-riddled baritone, and she knew it was far more likely when she was in front of the woman from her fantasies.

"Good. I was wondering if you could help me find a video."

Violet nodded. She still held her book in her hands, her thumbs acting as a bookmark. This close to the woman, she could now see small lines around her mouth and eyes. Before, she had seemed ageless, as if nothing had changed since the moment her body was captured on screen.

The film must have been at least ten years old, though. Violet had seen it when she was fifteen—far too young to be viewing materials of that content—but the VHS already had the worn cover edges and clipped sections that a well-loved movie obtained. Violet was twenty-three now; the same age, she believed, as the woman on the screen eight years earlier.

Violet's heart could not stop pounding. Her book shook. And the woman finally seemed to notice her stunned silence.

"Are you all right?"

"Yes," Violet said. A crack. A deeper pitch. Violet bit the inside of her mouth and tried again. "Yeah, I'm okay. It's just... I know you."

The woman tilted her head. For a second, her eyes betrayed her fear as she discovered what Violet meant. She'd seen the film—which meant that she'd seen her naked, completely open and vulnerable—but also that Violet had seen the ending of the film. It wasn't just a VHS porn flick that Violet had found in the bottom of a box in her uncle's basement. It was a porn film that had been taped from something else, the original source Violet wouldn't even discover until six years later, when she took this job first out of high school, and found the original in the back.

"I see," the woman said. "Okay. Well. This actually might be good."

"Why?"

"Because that's the film I'm looking for. The one where... you know. You saw me."

"I saw you..." Violet stopped and started several times. "Forgive me for being forward, but... I thought you were dead."

The woman smiled, just barely. Violet was struck by her green eyes. Violet had always thought they looked brown in the movie. Each thought comparing the filmic version of the woman to her real life counterpart, here in the flesh and very much not dead, made Violet's palms sweat and her body tense. If not for the estrogen already working its way through her body, and the tucking she'd done that morning, she'd be hard. It was only a look, but she felt like the fifteen year old boy she'd been when she first discovered the film. And then the nineteen year old who realized that the woman he had been keeping in his mind since he was fifteen was actually murdered at the end of the movie. Violet had only watched the snuff film once before sliding the VHS back into a box and hiding it where no one would find it. The woman that he had loved—named Violet according to the film's label—had made him question everything he thought he knew about himself and the world.

A year later, he was now *she* and going by Violet.

At the time, Violet thought naming herself after the snuffed out woman was the only way to keep the image of her alive.

But she was alive. Now faced with her dream woman, Violet wasn't sure what to do.
She glanced around the store to be sure no one needed help, but everything and everyone was fine. The back booths were booming with business and the older man in the anal section was completely content. No one noticed the beautiful woman because there were a dozen more just like her in front of them; no one was having an existential crisis because no one else here was trans and had constructed their entire identity around this moment.

No one here gave a damn.

"Can we talk somewhere?" the woman asked. "I think this is a better conversation to have over a drink, don't you think?"

When Violet remained quiet, the woman leaned closer. She placed a hand over Violet's book, cascading her fingers down the spine. Violet swallowed hard, suppressing her desire and revulsion at the woman's gory death on screen. She blinked once, saw the static and the glitch-y images, and then opened to see the woman, like Venus reborn, in front of her. She almost glowed.

"Yes. I think that's a good idea. Let me close up."

Violet stood from behind the counter. She closed down the booths at the back, angering some of the men in the process. The internet was still a new thing, still something that most of the older generation hadn't quite realized the potential of, and so the shop was still filled with people who would much rather view in private booths. Violet knew these men were a dying breed. *Back Door Rentals* had managed to contend with the DVD craze, but it would not survive the internet age. Suddenly, all desire to even work at *Back Door Rentals* disappeared. Violet now had what she always wanted: the woman that made her a woman.

Once the store was clear, she walked back over to the woman. She stood taller now, her winter jacket unbuttoned. Underneath she wore a black v-neck shirt and Tommy Hilfiger jeans. Violet was sure she had the same ones at home.

"You ready?"

The woman nodded. Violet led her to the concrete stairs and locked the final door.

"What should I call you?" Violet asked. "I realize now that you may have been using a name all those years ago."

The woman smiled and shook her head. "I'm Violet. Just like the tape said. And you are?"

Violet smiled, mirroring her namesake. "Exactly the same."

*

Five minutes into their coffee, Violet from the video insisted on being called "Vi." It was less confusing for Violet, and it also made her feel like an insider. She was already calling her dream woman by a nickname;

143

already creating the subtle bonds of intimacy between them that she'd craved so long ago.

"How much do you know?" Vi asked. She held her black coffee close to her body, using both hands around the mug. Her nails were painted red. Violet wondered if she had the same shade.

"I don't know much beyond what was on screen. You inside a red room. And then you inside a black one. Where you were, you know."

Vi nodded. On the back of Violet's eyelids, from ages fifteen to nineteen, the movie had just been the red section. Vi was on an examination table and a man in a doctor's uniform was removing her clothing. They fucked. There were more positions, more than Violet could dream up as a fifteen year old boy without access to the internet. Back then, she didn't even have access to nudie magazines because she'd been an only child with no father. Vi's breasts were the first ones she'd seen.

And she'd fallen in love with them. The red room was the entire movie to Violet and she'd watched it forwards and backwards. When she'd gotten to *Back Door* Rentals, she'd found the original film that was merely labeled VIOLET in large letters. The red room went to the black room, where Vi's throat was cut as she laid on a bed, bleeding out into the sheets.

Violet had stared at the screen in horror.

Then, with a sick feeling in her stomach, she rewound the tape to the beginning and watched it all the way through. Vi's death occurred three more times before she took the movie from the store.

Violet tried to explain her history with the movie in fewer words and with less focus on how arousing it had been--and more talk of how horrified. Vi didn't seem to care either way. Her gaze fixated and she leaned even closer

"So you watched two movies of me?"

Violet nodded.

"Were they both on VHS?"

Another nod.

"And were they originals?"

"What do you mean 'originals'?"

"They weren't studio movies, obviously. They could be tapped over."

Violet remembered learning the difference as a kid; the movies you could tape over had a small latch at the front of the tape that wasn't pushed in, while all of her other films—like the Disney ones—had the latched pushed in. It was a subtle way to signal to the VCR what was okay to use to tape *Dynasty* or *SNL* and what was not. Violet struggled to remember the porn movies.

"I think the first one—the red room one—was a studio movie. But I don't think the second one was."

"Good, good. I need the second one, then. The one with black room."

Violet bit her lip. "Do you... do you really want it? I mean, it's pretty gruesome. Horrible and misogynistic and—"

"But it's *me*. You're forgetting that. I acted in those scenes."

Violet made a face and tried to hide it with her coffee. Could it really be acting? She thought for so long that Vi was dead. It was why she had transitioned; why she had taken the name she did. If the woman who embodied femininity was gone, then nothing was sacred.

And she could step into the role and be just another intimation of the pure greatness that had come before. Vi was a Platonic ideal—always to strive for, but never reach.

When a cafe worker came by, she nearly bumped into Vi as she set down more coffee for Violet. Violet was about to complain, but the waitress was gone. Vi's mug was empty—she had gotten no refill—but she didn't seem to care. She stared into the empty mug, then at Violet, her gaze harsh.

"You're not protecting me from the film by not letting me have it. It's quite the opposite, actually."

"What do you mean?"

Vi sighed. She glanced around the cafe before leaning in close. For a moment, Violet wondered if the table between them was going to disappear, and their bodies would merge entirely together like an ink blot or kaleidoscopic reel.

"I found it online," Vi said. "I saw myself being murdered over and over again. I don't want that anymore."

"If it's online, it's online. Get the host to take it down."

"It doesn't work like that. And it's not the same thing. I could stand having the sex stuff up there. It was annoying, but I made that decision. The murder, though..." She shook her head. "I hate knowing it's out there."

"And it looks so real." Violet remembered the colour of the blood. The way it coagulated. What Vi's throat looked like as nothing but a wound. It was impossible to not stare at her neck now and wonder where the scar was. Violet gestured to her own throat with a shrug. "I still don't understand. You know..." Vi shrugged. "Movie magic."

"Hmmm." The explanation didn't fulfill Violet's need for knowledge. It became a void inside of her, a chasm that seemed like it would never be filled. "What will having the original film give you? It's still out there. I hate to break it to you, but the internet's going to change things. You're not going to be able to get your image back."

"But I can."

Vi leaned back suddenly. The space between them split in two. Violet felt it like a wound.

"I met this guy," Vi went on. "He actually recognized me from the movie. He said I could reclaim what I've lost. I just need the original VHS tape. I give that to him and I get a second chance."

"I think he's feeding you lies. I don't think it's possible to get back what you've lost. Not in that way."

"But you do believe in second chances, right? I mean, look at you."

Violet bit the side of her mouth. She wondered what part of her image gave away her trans status. Was it her chin? Her prone throat? She'd tried to

obscure her Adam's apple with a high collar on her
winter jacket, but that jacket that now was on the back
of her chair. Was it her thin hair? Her height of 5'9?
Her hands? All the obvious answers came to her, but
she knew deep down it was her voice. She always
passed in the store, at the bank, even at her college
night school classes—until she spoke.

Violet was about to ask what the hell her life had
to do with any of this, when she stopped herself. It had
absolutely everything. And Vi knew it. More than just
her voice, Vi saw the way in which Violet had modelled
herself on her older filmic image. Most trans women
do have a proxy; Madonna or Lauren Bacall, the
Hollywood image that fed their identity into as a child.
Violet never had that fracture of self until Vi came
along and died in front of her.

"Do you even have the movie?" Vi asked, her
voice hot and accusatory. "Or are you just wasting my
time right now and trying to get off in the process?"

"No." Violet shook her head, her voice steady. "No.
I have it. I just never wanted anyone else to see it. So I
hid it in my apartment. I hid it away from everyone."

"I appreciate that. But it's online now. There's no
hiding it. There's only destroying it. And this guy will
help."

"I still don't understand."

"Then come with me," Vi said. Her green eyes
pleaded. For a brief second, Violet thought they turned
brown, like they had on the screen. But it was only a
flicker of her nostalgia soaked imagination.
She swallowed back the last of her coffee and nodded.
"Okay. I'll come."

*

The man's name was Gerry. He lived across the
hall from Vi's apartment on the East Side of
Vancouver. Violet recognized the area from the few
times she visited the clinic to find doctors who would
prescribe her hormones. She hated the area; the
atmosphere always felt so unsafe, especially as
women seemed to drop like flies from either heroine or
men with knives. She realized now, as she snaked her

147

way up several flights of stairs to Gerry's place, that she had avoided the area because she always thought this was where Violet had died. She had gotten into the wrong car and the wrong studio and thought she was making a movie for fun. For a couple handfuls of cash she could do what she wanted with, but ended up paying for her life.

"Why was the movie made?" Violet asked.

Vi was ahead of her, her thick boots echoing as they walked up the stairwell. "Why do you think porn is made?"

"No. I mean... why the fake murder?"

"Again, why do you think people make snuff films?"

"To get people off. Fine. But it was fake. I always thought they were real. It was scary because it was real."

"Sex is real on the screen. And the death is real. But it's also not. I fuck someone, and they go inside of me, but I don't let myself stay there mentally. I go somewhere else. It's the same for the snuff stuff too." Violet wasn't exactly sure how a knife could go into someone and not have it affect them later. Without a scar on Vi's body, though, that seemed to be what had happened.

"Exactly how many have you made?" Violent asked. "I thought it was just the one?"

"We're here." Vi held open the door to the fifth floor. Violet's lungs already felt pressed against her chest from all the walking. She followed Vi down a hallway and to an apartment that seemed to radiate the sweet smell of smoke. Her previous question was left unanswered as Vi knocked on the door. A snake-like ornament, going in a circle, hung on the centre of the door.

"It's an ouroborous," Vi said before Gerry game to the door.

Gerry was a large man, taller than both of them, with a thick beard. He wore all black and had a shaved head. His smile split his round face in two as he shook Vi's hand. He then turned to examine Violet with a tilt to his head. It was a familiar action; the same one Vi had done when she'd assessed her in the store.

"I know you," he said.

"I work at *Back Door Rental*."

"Ah. That'd be it. Do we have the video?"

Vi nodded. She led the way into the dark apartment, Violet coming up at the heels. She held the original video in her winter jacket pocket. They'd stopped at her place before taking a cab out to the East Side. When she'd come back out with the video, Vi had looked at her with a sultry expression. It struck Violet harder than a punch to her gut. For a moment, she'd been convinced that they were going to skip everything and fuck on her bed.

But the moment had passed. Now, inside Gerry's apartment, the smell of cigarette smoke mixed with sage. He spoke at a rapid-fire pace, mostly asking Vi how she was doing and how her brothers and sisters were. Vi brushed off his questions and quickly turned to Violet.

"The tape?"

"Yes. The tape. Let's get to work."

Gerry's stare met hers. Violet paused. She clasped her hand around the edge of the VHS, not wanting to let it go. The storyline was so worn into her brain. "I want to know how it works."

Gerry sighed. He kicked back a chair at his kitchen table and gestured for everyone to sit down. Though it was hot inside the apartment, Violet kept her coat on as she sat. Gerry lit a cigarette before he talked, ashing it in between statements.

"You know that old story of a photograph taking your soul?" When Violet nodded, he went on. "It's bunk. Humans don't really have souls. But there is something to be said for digital copies of ourselves. It gets weaker, less potent, as the image proliferates. It's one of the reasons why certain art objects have such a high... oh, I don't know, radiance to them? It has nothing to do with the artist or even the paint they use. It's all about how many images of an image there are. Take Van Gogh." He said the name like *Hoff* instead of the more popular *Go*. "We see Starry Night everywhere and it's boring. Even when we see the original, it's kind of boring. We see more details, sure, and we see the texture of the paint, and it's better. But the object has no power anymore. It's too common."

"Okay," Violet said. "I get that. But what about pornography? Snuff films? I don't understand why you want this tape of Vi."

"She wants it. She wants her life back."

"She won't get it. Once you make a decision like this, it's permanent."

Gerry sucked extra long on the cigarette. He leaned closer. "Are you sure about that?"

"Well, I would assume so. Decisions only go one way."

"No, they don't. Let's take Van Gogh again. We hate Starry Night. We've seen it too much. So how about we get rid of it? We can't just throw away the postcards with the image on it. We have to destroy the original. And once we do, it's gone."

Violet was about to open her mouth to disagree, but Gerry spoke again.

"The structure of it remains, I will give you that. We know that something used to be on that wall. A man painted something about stars in the night. We try to remember and replace it. Sure. But that original is gone. And the rest will fade."

"And you think that will happen to Vi? She will fade?"

"I want to," Vi said.

Gerry gave her a sympathetic look before he turned his focus back on Violet. "We need to get rid of the source. The memory will still be there, and something else will come and try to fill the hollow structure of what's leftover. Pornography will always exist. And whether we like it or not, snuff films will too. Even if the death captured can be reversed in some way."

"I still don't understand," Violet said. The tape now felt hot in her hands. She traced her finger along the line that had the button. If she could press it in, then the tape would never be taped over. She hovered above it.

"All the things that came from this tape, good and bad, will still be there," Gerry said. "But weaker. It'll be like an empty glass. Still a glass, but you'll have to fill it again yourself."
Violet felt sadness swell in her throat. She wanted to keep the tape because she was on the tape. Vi was her and she was Violet. She wanted to become the epitome of womanhood when she saw it destroyed. If death wasn't death and even sex could be undone on screen, then did it leave her as an empty shell? A blank tape?

Violet pushed down the button. The movie would not be taped over. It would remain, static. And she handed it over.

Gerry's smile left his face as soon as he saw what she'd done. Vi's eyes widened. She looked from the tape to Gerry and then back at Violet.

"What did you do?"

"Nothing. I just want to stay a little while longer."

*

When Vi came into the video store next, she wore a red dress. Her hair was long and hung down in rivulets towards her waist. Gerry came in behind her. He ushered the people in the store out up the concrete steps as Vi made her way to the counter.

"We should talk," she said, voice long and smooth.

They had not seen one another in two weeks, not since the incident in the apartment. Violet had left after she gave back the tape and not uttered another word. Even if they would not be able to tape over the image, Violet figured they could have always unfurled everything from inside. Smashed it with a hammer, or run it over with a car. Destruction was as plentiful as the type of porn to pick from. Always so many options.

Meanwhile, Violet tried to go on with her life. But she felt herself fading. Even if the tape's image remained protected, the illusion in her mind had been shattered. Vi was a real person with a real life; the tape was a fake. Not even death was real anymore.

151

"Where do you want to talk?" Violet asked.

"Back room, maybe?"

Violet nodded. She opened the back room where most of the old movies were kept. Jason, the owner who was never around, sometimes had toys back there too. A cot for when they had to do inventory and wanted to sit down. Jason was determined to expand the store beyond films, especially because of the internet, but Violet knew he would fail. The boxes of the merchandise seemed static next to the movies and DVDs that were taking up space.

Gerry followed them to the back. He pulled a camcorder out of his backpack and kept it rolling. Violet was about to ask what was going on, but Vi kissed her. Her mouth was hard, jagged. Violet's body reacted through sense-memory and basic response. Vi kissed her like she'd been kissed on screen. She ran her hands up and down Violet's body like she had seen on screen.

When they fell on the cot, it was exactly like it had been in the red room scenes. Violet leaned back as Vi disrobed her with the precision of a doctor. Not even Violet's mismatched sex made her feel nervous or uncomfortable. The movie scene played out as if it was always there, always permanent.

Violet felt herself come back to life. She was no longer fading, but existing in bold colours. Not every section of the film was the same—two women now instead of a man and a woman—but the structure was the same. The structure was what mattered; it was the heart of the event. When Violet came, the scene etched itself in her memory.

Then came time for the last section, the one in the black room.

Gerry handed Vi a knife. Violet remained naked, prone. Fear percolated in the base of her stomach, next to desire. She wanted this. She was this. She'd been made in this image and now she was going to become it. Like a great art object—the original.

    Vi walked over to her, knife ready. Gerry continued to film. Violet extended her neck, waiting to become herself all over again.

***

©2018 Evelyn Deshane

FAHRENHEIT '13
AN IMPRINT OF FAHREHEIT PRESS

RISING FROM THE ASHES OF THE MUCH LOVED NUMBER THIRTEEN PRESS - FAHRENHEIT 13 IS A NEW IMPRINT FROM PUNK NOIR VETERANS FAHRENHEIT PRESS.

NOIR LEGEND CHRIS BLACK IS INSTALLED AS EDITOR IN CHIEF AND IS ACCEPTING SUBMISSIONS NOW

F13NOIR@FAHRENHEIT-PRESS.COM

FAHRENHEIT 13 WILL RE-PUBLISHING ALL OF THE ORIGINAL NUMBER THIRTEEN PRESS NOVELLAS AS WELL AS COMMISSIONING AWESOME NEW CRIME FICTION FROM ALL AROUND THE WORLD.

PULP ★ CRIME ★ NOIR

WWW.FAHRENHEIT-PRESS.COM

@FAHRENHEITPRESS   @F13NOIR

A PAUL WRIGHT PICTURE
5 SHELLS
BEAUTIFUL...
VISUALLY STRIKING...
SOLID PERFORMANCES...
A DAMN GOOD FILM.
- DARK OF THE MATINEE
THERE IS NO HOME

TOUGH

a journal of crime fiction and occasional reviews

www.toughcrime.com

QUALITY
CHEAP
THRILLS
T R Bottom PRESS
DEEP EAST TEXAS
ECONO
CLASH
review
#TWO
EDITED BY: J.D. GRAVES
ECONOCLASH.COM

larquepress.com

Author Bios & Acknowledgements

George Garnet's short fiction has appeared in *Mystery Weekly, The Dark City Crime and Mystery Magazine, eFiction, The Literary Hatchet, Heater, Romance Magazine, Needle in the Hay, The Lady in the Loft, GKBC* and elsewhere.

Aidan Thorn is from Southampton, England. In September 2015 *Number 13 Press* published Aidan's first novella, "When the Music's Over", this book was re-realeased in 2018 by *Fahrenheit 13*. December 2018 will mark the release of Aidan's second novella, "Rival Sons" by *Shotgun Honey*. His short fiction has appeared in *Byker Books Radgepacket* series, *Near to the Knuckle* Anthologies: *Gloves Off* and *Rogue, Exiles: An Outsider Anthology, The Big Adios Western Digest* and *Shadows & Light, Hardboiled Dames and Sin*, as well as online in numerous mags. and ezines. In 2016 Aidan collated and edited the charity anthology, *Paladins*.

Rex Weiner's "The (Original) Adventures of Ford Fairlane" will be published for the first time in July 2018 by *Rare Bird Books*. As a journalist, Rex Weiner's articles have appeared in *Vanity Fair, The Paris Review, The New Yorker, LA Weekly, L'Officiel Hommes*, and *Rolling Stone Italia*. He is one of the founding editors of *High Times Magazine* and a former editor of *Swank* ("The Magazine For Men"). Weiner's screen credits include *The Adventures of Ford Fairlane*, based on his original stories, directed by Renny Harlin and starring Andrew Dice Clay for 20th Century Fox. As one of the first writers brought on board to launch the TV series *Miami Vice*, Weiner wrote the now classic 9th episode, "Glades."

John Bosworth lives in Seattle and can be found on Twitter @JGBosworth

Mike Payne's credits include Pseudopod.org and *Sanitarium Magazine*.

Jim Thomsen is a writer and editor whose short crime fiction has been published in *Shotgun Honey*, *Pulp Modern* and *West Coast Crime Wave*. A former newspaper reporter and editor, he lives in his hometown of Bainbridge Island, Washington when he isn't drifting around somewhere else in a broke-dick car.

E.F. Sweetman is a writer living in Beverly, Massachusetts. Her short stories have been published in *Microchondria II* and *One Night in Salem*, and *Switchblade V* In addition to writing short stories, she also working on a noir novel. She lives with her husband, sons, and two very bad terriers. When she is not writing, you can find her glaring out the windows at her neighbors.

Travis Richardson has been a finalist for the Macavity, Anthony and Derringer short story awards and was listed in *2017* Best *American Mystery Stories*. His novella *Lost* in *Clover* was listed in Spinetingler Magazine's Best Crime Fiction of 2012. His second novella, *Keeping the Record*, came out in 2014. He has published stories in crime fiction publications such as *Thuglit*, *Shotgun Honey*, *The Flash Fiction Offensive*, and the anthology, *The Obama Inheritance*. He reviewed Anton Chekhov short stories at http://www.chekhovshorts.com and plans to publish a short story collection later this year. http://www.tsrichardson.com

Rusty Barnes has been published widely in journals like *Plots With Guns*, *Manslaughter Review*, and Bull. His latest novel is called *Knuckledragger*, published by Shotgun *Honey*/*Down & Out Books*. His next novel, *The Last Danger*, will appear in October 2018.

Scot Carpenter grew up on a ranch in central Texas. At various times he's worked as a maintenance man, welder, blacksmith, sales clerk and teacher while living in a dozen different states and spending entirely too much time messing about in boats and supporting bars. He's the author of the novel, *Crossing the* Bloodline and a contributor to the short story collection, *The Sharpened Quill*, both available from Amazon. He currently lives in Arizona.

Danny Sophabmisay is a janitor at MIT who solves complex math equations written on blackboards. He is a repeat offender in *Switchblade*.

Tom Barlow is an Ohio writer. Other stories of his may be found in anthologies including *Best American Mystery Stories 2013*, *Dames and Sin* and *Plan B Omnibus* and periodicals including *Switchblade* (yay!), *Red Room*, *Pulp Modern*, *Heater*, *Plots With Guns*, *Mystery Weekly*, *Needle*, *Thuglit*, *Manslaughter Review* and *Tough*. His novel "I'll Meet You Yesterday" from *Bundoran Press* and short story collection "Welcome to the Goat Rodeo" from *Pagespring Press* are available on Amazon.

Tais Teng is a Dutch writer and illustrator. He started out as Thijs van Ebbenhorst Tengbergen which is clearly too long to leave room on the cover for a damsel in distress. He likes writing crime stories, ranging all the way from rather humorous occult detectives to deeply noir. With his longtime writing mate Jaap Boekestein he is working on a Yakuza novel set in an alternate Japan. Most recent crime sales are to *Tokyo* Yakuza, *Switchblade*, *Midnight Hour* and *Black Cat Mystery Magazine*

Evelyn Deshane's creative and nonfiction work has appeared in *Plenitude Magazine*, Briarpatch *Magazine*, *Strange Horizons*, *Lackington's*, and *Bitch Magazine*, among other publications. Evelyn (pron. Eve-a-lyn) received an MA from Trent University and is currently completing a PhD at the University of Waterloo. Evelyn's most recent project #Trans is an edited collection about transgender and nonbinary identity online. Follow @evelyndeshane or visit evedeshane.wordpress.com for more info.

Special Thanks to cover model **Demi Cobar**, **The Shamrock Social Club**, **Eric Beetner** and **S.W. Lauden** of the *Writer Types* podcast, for their continued support of *Switchblade*.

Made in the USA
San Bernardino, CA
24 September 2018